ALSO BY CHIMAMANDA NGOZI ADICHIE

Half of a Yellow Sun

Purple Hibiscus

THE THING AROUND YOUR NECK

THE
THING AROUND YOUR NECK

•

Chimamanda Ngozi Adichie

Alfred A. Knopf   New York   Toronto   2009

FIC
Adichie

This Is a Borzoi Book
Published by Alfred A. Knopf
and Alfred A. Knopf Canada

Copyright © 2009 by Chimamanda Ngozi Adichie

All rights reserved. Published in the United States by Alfred A. Knopf,
a division of Random House, Inc., New York, and in Canada by
Alfred A. Knopf Canada, a division of Random House of Canada
Limited, Toronto.
www.aaknopf.com
www.randomhouse.ca

Owing to limitations of space, previous publication
information appears on page 223.

Knopf, Borzoi Books, and the colophon are registered trademarks
of Random House, Inc.
Knopf Canada and colophon are trademarks.

Library of Congress Cataloging-in-Publication Data
Adichie, Chimamanda Ngozi, [date]
    The thing around your neck / Chimamanda Ngozi Adichie.—
1st ed.
    p. cm.
ISBN 978-0-307-27107-5
1. Short stories, Nigerian (English) 2. Nigeria—Fiction. I. Title.
PR 9387.9.A34354T55 2009
823'.92—dc22 2008041271

Library and Archives Canada Cataloguing in Publication
Adichie, Chimamanda Ngozi, 1977–
The thing around your neck / Chimamanda Ngozi Adichie.
ISBN 978-0-307-39789-8
I. Title.
PR9387.9.A34354T45 2009   823'.92   C2008-907089-5

Manufactured in the United States of America
First North American Edition

For Ivara

CONTENTS

THE THING AROUND YOUR NECK

CELL ONE

The first time our house was robbed, it was our neighbor Osita who climbed in through the dining room window and stole our TV, our VCR, and the *Purple Rain* and *Thriller* videotapes my father had brought back from America. The second time our house was robbed, it was my brother Nnamabia who faked a break-in and stole my mother's jewelry. It happened on a Sunday. My parents had traveled to our hometown, Mbaise, to visit our grandparents, so Nnamabia and I went to church alone. He drove my mother's green Peugeot 504. We sat together in church as we usually did, but we did not nudge each other and stifle giggles about somebody's ugly hat or threadbare caftan, because Nnamabia left without a word after about ten minutes. He came back just before the priest said, "The Mass is ended. Go in peace." I was a little piqued. I imagined he had gone off to smoke and to see some girl, since he had the car to himself for once, but he could at least have told me where he was going. We drove home in silence and, when he parked in our long driveway, I stopped to pluck some ixora flowers while Nnamabia unlocked the front door. I went inside to find him standing still in the middle of the parlor.

"We've been robbed!" he said in English.

It took me a moment to understand, to take in the scattered room. Even then, I felt that there was a theatrical quality to the way the drawers were flung open, as if it had been done by somebody who wanted to make an impression on the discoverers. Or perhaps it was simply that I knew my brother so well. Later, when my parents came home and neighbors began to troop in to say *ndo,* and to snap their fingers and heave their shoulders up and down, I sat alone in my room upstairs and realized what the queasiness in my gut was: Nnamabia had done it, I knew. My father knew, too. He pointed out that the window louvers had been slipped out from the inside, rather than outside (Nnamabia was really much smarter than that; perhaps he had been in a hurry to get back to church before Mass ended), and that the robber knew exactly where my mother's jewelry was—the left corner of her metal trunk. Nnamabia stared at my father with dramatic, wounded eyes and said, "I know I have caused you both terrible pain in the past, but I would never violate your trust like this." He spoke English, using unnecessary words like "terrible pain" and "violate," as he always did when he was defending himself. Then he walked out through the back door and did not come home that night. Or the next night. Or the night after. He came home two weeks later, gaunt, smelling of beer, crying, saying he was sorry and he had pawned the jewelry to the Hausa traders in Enugu and all the money was gone.

"How much did they give you for my gold?" my mother asked him. And when he told her, she placed both hands on her head and cried, "Oh! Oh! *Chi m egbuo m!* My God has killed me!" It was as if she felt that the least he could have done was get a good price. I wanted to slap her. My father asked Nnamabia to write a report: how he had sold the jewelry, what he had spent the money on, with whom he had spent it. I didn't think Nnamabia would tell the truth, and I don't think my father thought he would, either, but he liked reports, my professor father, he liked things written down and nicely documented. Besides, Nnamabia was seventeen, with a carefully tended beard. He was in that space between secondary school and university and was too old for caning. What else could my father have done? After Nnamabia wrote the report, my father filed it in the steel drawer in his study where he kept our school papers.

"That he could hurt his mother like this" was the last thing my father said, in a mutter.

But Nnamabia really hadn't set out to hurt her. He did it because my mother's jewelry was the only thing of any value in the house: a lifetime's collection of solid gold pieces. He did it, too, because other sons of professors were doing it. This was the season of thefts on our serene Nsukka campus. Boys who had grown up watching *Sesame Street,* reading Enid Blyton, eating cornflakes for breakfast, attending the university staff primary school in smartly polished brown sandals, were now cutting through the mosquito netting of their neighbors' windows, sliding out glass louvers, and climbing in to steal TVs and VCRs. We knew the thieves. Nsukka campus was such a small place— the houses sitting side by side on tree-lined streets, separated only by low hedges—that we could not but know who was stealing. Still, when their professor parents saw one another at the staff club or at church or at a faculty meeting, they continued to moan about riffraff from town coming onto their sacred campus to steal.

The thieving boys were the popular ones. They drove their parents' cars in the evening, their seats pushed back and their arms stretched out to reach the steering wheel. Osita, the neighbor who had stolen our TV only weeks before the Nnamabia incident, was lithe and handsome in a brooding sort of way and walked with the grace of a cat. His shirts were always sharply ironed; I used to look across the hedge and see him and close my eyes and imagine that he was walking toward me, coming to claim me as his. He never noticed me. When he stole from us, my parents did not go over to Professor Ebube's house to ask him to ask his son to bring back our things. They said publicly that it was riffraff from town. But they knew it was Osita. Osita was two years older than Nnamabia; most of the thieving boys were a little older than Nnamabia, and perhaps that was why Nnamabia did not steal from another person's house. Perhaps he did not feel old enough, qualified enough, for anything bigger than my mother's jewelry.

Nnamabia looked just like my mother, with that honey-fair complexion, large eyes, and a generous mouth that curved perfectly. When my mother took us to the market, traders would call out, "Hey! Madam, why did you waste your fair skin on a boy and leave the girl so dark? What is a boy doing with all this beauty?" And my mother would chuckle, as though she took a mischievous and joyful responsibility for Nnamabia's good looks. When, at eleven, Nnamabia broke the window of his classroom with a stone, my mother gave him the money to replace it and did not tell my father. When he lost some library books in class two, she told his form-mistress that our houseboy had stolen them. When, in class three, he left early every day to attend catechism and it turned out he never once went and so could not receive Holy Communion, she told the other parents that he had malaria on the examination day. When he took the key of my father's car and pressed it into a piece of soap that my father found before Nnamabia could take it to a locksmith, she made vague sounds about how he was just experimenting and it didn't mean a thing. When he stole the exam questions from the study and sold them to my father's students, she shouted at him but then told my father that Nnamabia was sixteen, after all, and really should be given more pocket money.

I don't know whether Nnamabia felt remorse for stealing her jewelry. I could not always tell from my brother's gracious, smiling face what it was he really felt. And we did not talk about it. Even though my mother's sisters sent her their gold earrings, even though she bought an earring-and-pendant set from Mrs. Mozie, the glamorous woman who imported gold from Italy, and began to drive to Mrs. Mozie's house once a month to pay for it in installments, we never talked, after that day, about Nnamabia's stealing her jewelry. It was as if pretending that Nnamabia had not done the things he had done would give him the opportunity to start afresh. The robbery might never have been mentioned again if Nnamabia had not been arrested three years later, in his third year in the university, and locked up at the police station.

It was the season of cults on our serene Nsukka campus. It was the time when signboards all over the university read, in bold letters, SAY NO TO CULTS. The Black Axe, the Buccaneers, and the Pirates were the best known. They may once have been benign fraternities, but they had evolved and were now called "cults"; eighteen-year-olds who had mastered the swagger of American rap videos were undergoing secret and strange initiations that sometimes left one or two of them dead on Odim Hill. Guns and tortured loyalties and axes had become common. Cult wars had become common: a boy would leer at a girl who turned out to be the girlfriend of the Capone of the Black Axe, and that boy, as he walked to a kiosk to buy a cigarette later, would be stabbed in the thigh, and he would turn out to be a member of the Buccaneers, and so his fellow

Buccaneers would go to a beer parlor and shoot the nearest Black Axe boy in the shoulder, and then the next day a Buccaneer member would be shot dead in the refectory, his body falling against aluminum bowls of soup, and that evening a Black Axe boy would be hacked to death in his room in a lecturer's Boys' Quarters, his CD player splattered with blood. It was senseless. It was so abnormal that it quickly became normal. Girls stayed inside their hostel rooms after lectures and lecturers quivered and when a fly buzzed too loudly, people were afraid. So the police were called in. They sped across campus in their rickety blue Peugeot 505, rusty guns poking out of the car windows, and glowered at the students. Nnamabia came home from his lectures laughing. He thought the police would have to do better; everyone knew the cult boys had more modern guns.

My parents watched Nnamabia's laughing face with silent concern and I knew that they, too, were wondering whether he was in a cult. Sometimes I thought he was. Cult boys were popular and Nnamabia was very popular. Boys yelled out his nickname—"The Funk!"—and shook his hand whenever he passed by, and girls, especially the popular Big Chicks, hugged him for too long when they said hello. He went to all the parties, the tame ones on campus and the wilder ones in town, and he was the kind of ladies' man who was also a guy's guy, the kind who smoked a pack of Rothmans a day and was reputed to be able to finish a carton of Star beer in a sitting. Other times I thought he was not in a cult, because he *was* so popular and it seemed more his style that he would befriend all the different cult boys and be the enemy of none. And I was not entirely sure, either, that my brother had whatever it took—guts or insecurity—to join a cult. The only time I asked him if he was in a cult, he looked at me with surprise, his eyelashes long and thick, as if I should have known better than to ask, before he said, "Of course not." I believed him. My father believed him, too. But our believing him made little difference, because he had already been arrested and accused of belonging to a cult. He told me this—"Of course not"—on our first visit to the police station where he was locked up.

This is how it happened. On a humid Monday, four cult members waited at the campus gate and waylaid a professor driving a red Mercedes. They pressed a gun to her head, shoved her out of the car, and drove it to the Faculty of Engineering, where they shot three boys walking out of their lecture halls. It was noon. I was in a class nearby, and when we heard the sharp bangs, our lecturer was the first to run out of the room. There was loud screaming and suddenly the staircases were packed with scrambling students unsure in which direction to run. Outside, three bodies lay on the lawn. The red Mercedes had screeched away. Many students packed hasty bags and *okada* drivers charged twice the usual fare to take them to the motor park. The vice chancellor announced that all evening classes were canceled and everyone had to be indoors after 9 p.m. This did not make much sense to me, since the shooting happened in sparkling daylight, and perhaps it did not make sense to Nnamabia, either, because on the first day of the curfew, he was not home at 9 p.m. and did not come home that night. I assumed he had stayed at a friend's; he did not always come home anyway. The next morning, a security man came to tell my parents that Nnamabia had been arrested with some cult boys at a bar and had been taken away in a police van. My mother screamed, "*Ekwuzikwana!* Don't say that!" My father calmly thanked the security man. He drove us to the police station in town. There, a constable chewing on a dirty pen cover said, "You mean those cult boys arrested yesterday night? They have been taken to Enugu. Very serious case! We must stop this cult trouble once and for all!"

We got back into the car and a new fear gripped us all. Nsukka—our slow, insular campus and the slower, more insular town—was manageable; my father would know the police superintendent. But Enugu was anonymous, the state capital with the Mechanized Division of the Nigerian Army and the police headquarters and the traffic wardens at busy intersections. It was where the police could do what they were famed for when under pressure to produce results: kill people.

The Enugu police station was in a walled-around, sprawling compound full of buildings; dusty, damaged cars were piled by the gate, near the sign that said OFFICE OF THE COMMISSIONER OF POLICE. My father drove toward the rectangular bungalow at the other end of the compound. My mother bribed the two policemen at the desk with money and with *jollof* rice and meat, all tied up in a black waterproof bag, and they allowed Nnamabia to come out of his cell and sit on a bench with us under an umbrella tree. Nobody asked why he stayed out that night when he knew that a curfew had been imposed. Nobody said that the policemen were irrational to walk into a bar and arrest all the boys drinking there, as well as the barman. Instead we listened to Nnamabia talk. He sat straddling the wooden bench, a food flask of rice and chicken in front of him, his eyes brightly expectant: an entertainer about to perform.

"If we ran Nigeria like this cell," he said, "we would have no problems in this country. Things are so organized. Our cell has a chief called General Abacha and he has a second in command. Once you come in, you have to give them some money. If you don't, you're in trouble."

"And did you have any money?" my mother asked.

Nnamabia smiled, his face even more beautiful with a new pimple-like insect bite on his forehead, and said in Igbo that he had slipped his money into his anus shortly after the arrest at the bar. He knew the policemen would take it if he didn't hide it and he knew he would need it to buy his peace in the cell. He bit into a fried drumstick and switched to English. "General Abacha was impressed with how I hid my money. I've made myself amenable to him. I praise him all the time. When the men asked all of us newcomers to hold our ears and frog-jump to their singing, he let me go after ten minutes. The others had to do it for almost thirty minutes."

My mother hugged herself, as though she felt cold. My father said nothing, watching Nnamabia carefully. And I imagined him, my *amenable* brother, rolling one-hundred-naira notes into thin cigarette shapes and then slipping a hand into the back of his trousers to slide them painfully into himself.

Later, as we drove back to Nsukka, my father said, "This is what I should have done when he broke into the house. I should have had him locked up in a cell."

My mother stared silently out of the window.

"Why?" I asked.

"Because this has shaken him for once. Couldn't you see?" my father asked with a small smile. I couldn't see it. Not that day. Nnamabia seemed fine to me, slipping his money into his anus and all.

Nnamabia's first shock was seeing the Buccaneer sobbing. The boy was tall and tough, rumored to have carried out one of the killings, to be in line for Capone next semester, and yet there he was in the cell cowering and sobbing after the chief had given him a knock behind the head. Nnamabia told me this on our visit the following day, in a voice lined with both disgust and disappointment; it was as if he had suddenly been made to see that the Incredible Hulk was really just green paint. His second shock, a few days later, was Cell One, the cell beyond his. Two policemen had carried out a swollen dead man from Cell One and stopped by Nnamabia's cell to make sure the corpse was seen by all.

Even the chief of his cell seemed afraid of Cell One. When Nnamabia and his cell mates, those who could afford to buy bathing water in the plastic buckets that had once held paint, were let out to bathe in the open yard, the policemen watched them and often shouted, "Stop that or you are going to Cell One now!" Nnamabia had nightmares about Cell One. He could not imagine a place worse than his cell, which was so crowded he often stood pressed against the cracked wall. Tiny *kwalikwata* lived inside the cracks and their bites were vicious, and when he yelped his cell mates called him Milk and Banana Boy, University Boy, Yeye Fine Boy.

They were too tiny to bite so painfully, those bugs. The biting was worse during the night, when they all had to sleep on their sides, head to foot, except the chief with his whole back lavishly on the floor. It was the chief who shared the plates of *garri* and watery soup that were pushed into the cell everyday. Each person got two mouthfuls. Nnamabia told us this during the first week. As he spoke I wondered if the bugs in the wall had bitten his face, too, or if the bumps spreading all over his forehead had come from an infection. Some of them were tipped with pus the color of cream. He scratched at them as he said, "I had to shit in a waterproof bag today, standing up. The toilet was too full. They flush it only on Saturdays."

His tone was histrionic. I wanted to ask him to shut up, because he was enjoying his new role as the sufferer of indignities, and because he did not understand how lucky he was that the policemen allowed him to come out and eat our food, how stupid he'd been to stay out drinking that night, how uncertain his chances were of being released.

We visited him every day of the first week. We went in my father's old Volvo because my mother's older Peugeot 504 was considered unsafe for trips outside Nsukka. When we passed the police checkpoints on the road, I noticed that my parents were different—subtly so, but different. My father no longer delivered a monologue, as soon as we were waved on, on how illiterate and corrupt the police were. He did not bring up the day they had delayed us for an hour because he refused to bribe them, or the way they had stopped a bus in which my beautiful cousin Ogechi was traveling and singled her out and called her a whore because she had two cell phones and asked her for so much money that she knelt on the ground in the rain begging them to let her go since her bus had already been allowed to go. My mother did not mumble, They are symptoms of a larger malaise. Instead my parents remained silent. It was as if refusing to criticize the police as usual would somehow make Nnamabia's freedom imminent. "Delicate" was the word the superintendent at Nsukka had used. Getting Nnamabia out anytime soon would be delicate, especially with the police commissioner in Enugu giving gloating, preening interviews on television about the arrested cultists. The cult problem was serious. Big Men in Abuja were following events. Everybody wanted to appear to be doing something.

The second week, I told my parents we were not going to visit Nnamabia. We did not know how long we would have to keep doing this and petrol was too expensive to drive three hours every day and it would not hurt Nnamabia to fend for himself for a day.

My father looked at me, surprised, and asked, "What do you mean?" My mother eyed me up and down and headed for the door and said nobody was begging me to come; I could sit there and do nothing while my innocent brother suffered. She was walking toward the car and I ran after her, and when I got outside I was not sure what to do, so I picked up a stone near the ixora bush and hurled it at the windshield of the Volvo. The windshield cracked. I heard the brittle sound and saw the tiny lines spreading like rays on the glass before I turned and dashed upstairs and locked myself in my room to protect myself from my mother's fury. I heard her shouting. I heard my father's voice. Finally there was silence, and I did not hear the car start. Nobody went to see Nnamabia that day. It surprised me, this little victory.

We visited him the next day. We said nothing about the windshield, although the cracks had spread out like ripples on a frozen stream. The policeman at the desk, the pleasant dark-skinned one, asked why we had not come the day before; he had missed my mother's *jollof* rice. I expected Nnamabia to ask, too, even to be upset, but he looked oddly sober, an expression

I had not seen before. He did not eat all of his rice. He kept looking away, toward the cluster of half-burned cars at the end of the compound, the remnants of accidents.

"What is wrong?" my mother asked, and Nnamabia began to speak almost immediately, as if he had been waiting to be asked. His Igbo was even-toned, his voice neither rising nor falling. An old man had been pushed into his cell the day before, a man perhaps in his mid-seventies, white-haired, skin finely wrinkled, with the old-fashioned refinement of an incorruptible retired civil servant. His son was wanted for armed robbery, and when the police could not find the son, they decided to lock him up instead.

"The man did nothing," Nnamabia said.

"But you did nothing, too," my mother said.

Nnamabia shook his head as if she did not understand. In the following days, he was more subdued. He spoke less, and mostly about the old man: how he had no money and could not buy bathing water, how the other men made fun of him or accused him of hiding his son, how the chief ignored him, how he looked frightened and so terribly small.

"Does he know where his son is?" my mother asked.

"He has not seen his son in four months," Nnamabia said.

My father said something about how it was irrelevant whether or not the man knew where his son was.

"Of course," my mother said. "It is wrong, but this is what the police do all the time. If they do not find the person they are looking for, they will lock up his father or his mother or his relative."

My father brushed at something on his knee—an impatient gesture. He did not understand why my mother was stating the obvious.

"The man is ill," Nnamabia said. "His hands shake and shake, even when he's asleep."

My parents were silent. Nnamabia closed the food flask of rice and turned to my father. "I want to give him some of this, but if I bring it into the cell General Abacha will take it."

My father went over and asked the policeman at the desk if we could be allowed to see the old man in Nnamabia's cell for a few minutes. The policeman was the light-skinned, acerbic one who never said thank you when my mother handed over the rice and money bribe. Now he sneered in my father's face and said he could well lose his job for letting Nnamabia out and yet we were asking for another person to be allowed out? Did we think this was a boarding school visiting day? Didn't we know that this was a high-security holding place for criminal elements of society? My father came back and sat down with a sigh and Nnamabia silently scratched at his bumpy face.

The next day, Nnamabia barely touched his rice. He said that the policemen had splashed detergent water on the floor and walls of the cell in the name of cleaning as they usually did and that the old man, who could not afford water, who had not bathed in a week, had hurried into the cell and yanked his shirt off and rubbed his frail back against the detergent-wet floor. The policemen started to laugh when they saw him do this and they asked him to take all his clothes off and parade in the corridor outside the cell, and as he did they laughed louder and asked whether his son the thief knew that papa's penis was so shriveled. Nnamabia was staring at his yellow-orange rice as he spoke, and when he looked up I saw my brother's eyes fill with tears—my worldly brother—and I felt a tenderness for him that I could not have explained had I been asked to.

.   .   .

Two days later, there was another cult attack on campus: a boy hacked another boy with an axe right in front of the music department building.

"This is good," my mother said as she and my father got ready to go and see the Nsukka police superintendent again. "They cannot say now that they have arrested all the cult boys." We did not go to Enugu that day, because my parents spent so long at the superintendent's, but they came back with good news. Nnamabia and the barman were to be released immediately. One of the cult boys had become an informer, and he insisted that Nnamabia was not a member. We left earlier than usual in the morning, without *jollof* rice, the sun already so hot that all the car windows were down. My mother was jumpy on the drive. She was used to saying "*Nekwa ya!* Watch out!" to my father as if he could not see the cars making dangerous turns in the other lane, but this time she did it so often that just before we got to Ninth Mile, where hawkers crowded around the car with their trays of *okpa* and boiled eggs and cashew nuts, my father stopped the car and snapped, "Just who is driving this car, Uzoamaka?"

Inside the sprawling station compound, two policemen were flogging somebody who was lying on the ground under the umbrella tree. At first I thought, with a lurch in my chest, that it was Nnamabia, but it was not. I knew the boy who lay on the ground, writhing and shouting with each lash of a policeman's *koboko*. He was called Aboy, and he had the grave, ugly face of a hound and drove a Lexus on campus and was said to be a Buccaneer. I tried not to look at him as we walked into the station. The policeman on duty, the one with tribal marks on his cheeks who always said "God bless you" when he took his bribe, looked away when he saw us. Prickly hives spread over my skin. I knew then that something was wrong. My parents gave him the note from the superintendent. The policeman did not look at it. He knew about the release order, he told my father, the bar man had already been released but there was a complication with the boy. My mother began to shout. "The boy? What do you mean? Where is my son?"

The policeman got up. "I will call my senior to explain to you."

My mother rushed at him and pulled at his shirt. "Where is my son? Where is my son?" My father pried her away and the policeman brushed at his shirt, as if she had left some dirt there, before he turned to walk away.

"Where is our son?" my father asked in a voice so quiet, so steely, that the policeman stopped.

"They took him away, sir," he said.

"They took him away?" my mother broke in. She was still shouting. "What are you saying? Have you killed my son? Have you killed my son?"

"Where is he?" my father asked again in the same quiet voice. "Where is our son?"

"My senior said I should call him when you come," the policeman said, and this time he turned and hurried through a door.

It was after he left that I felt chilled by fear, that I wanted to run after him and like my mother pull at his shirt until he produced Nnamabia. The senior policeman came out and I searched his completely blank face for an expression.

"Good day, sir," he said to my father.

"Where is our son?" my father asked. My mother was breathing noisily. Later I would realize that at that moment each of us suspected privately that Nnamabia had been killed by trigger-happy policemen and that this man's job was to find the best lie to tell us about how he had died.

"No problem, sir. It is just that we transferred him. I will take you there right away." There was something nervous about the policeman; his face remained blank but he did not meet my father's eyes.

"Transferred him?"

"We got the release order this morning, but he had already been transferred. We don't have petrol, so I was waiting for you to come so that we go together to where he is."

"Where is he?"

"Another site. I will take you there."

"Why was he transferred?"

"I was not here, sir. They said he misbehaved yesterday and they took him to Cell One and then there was a transfer of all the people in Cell One to another site."

"He misbehaved? What do you mean?"

"I was not here, sir."

My mother spoke then in a broken voice. "Take me to my son! Take me to my son right now!"

I sat in the back with the policeman. He smelled of the kind of old camphor that seemed to last forever in my mother's trunk. We did not speak except for his giving my father directions until we arrived about fifteen minutes later, my father driving inordinately fast, as fast as my heart was beating. The small compound looked neglected, with patches of overgrown grass, with old bottles and plastic bags and paper strewn everywhere. The policeman hardly waited for my father to stop the car before he opened the door and hurried out, and again I felt chilled by fear. We were in this part of town with untarred roads and there had been no sign that said Police Station and there was a stillness in the air, a strange deserted feeling. But the policeman came out with Nnamabia. There he was, my handsome brother, walking toward us, unchanged, it seemed, until he came close enough for my mother to hug him and I saw him wince and back away; his left arm was covered in soft-looking welts. Dried blood was caked around his nose.

"Nna-Boy, why did they beat you like this?" my mother asked him. She turned to the policeman. "Why did you people do this to my son?"

The man shrugged, a new insolence to his demeanor; it was as if he had been uncertain about Nnamabia's well-being but now could let himself talk. "You cannot raise your children well, all of you people who feel important because you work in the university. When your children misbehave, you think they should not be punished. You are lucky, madam, very lucky that they released him."

My father said, "Let's go."

He opened the door and Nnamabia climbed in and we drove home. My father did not stop at any of the police checkpoints on the road; once, a policeman gestured threateningly with his gun as we sped past. The only thing my mother said on the silent drive was, Did Nnamabia want us to stop at Ninth Mile and buy some *okpa*? Nnamabia said no. We had arrived in Nsukka when he finally spoke.

"Yesterday the policemen asked the old man if he wanted a free bucket of water. He said yes. So they told him to take his clothes off and parade the corridor. My cell mates were laughing. But some of them said it was wrong to treat an old man like that." Nnamabia paused, his eyes distant. "I shouted at the policeman. I said the old man was innocent and ill and if they kept him here they would never find his son because he did not even know where his son was. They said I should shut up immediately or they would take me to Cell One. I didn't care. I didn't shut up. So they pulled me out and beat me and took me to Cell One."

Nnamabia stopped there and we asked him nothing else. Instead I imagined him raising his voice, calling the policeman a stupid idiot, a spineless coward, a sadist, a bastard, and I imagined the shock of the policemen, the shock of the chief staring openmouthed, the other cell mates stunned at the audacity of the handsome boy from the university. And I imagined the old man himself looking on with surprised pride and quietly refusing to undress. Nnamabia did not say what had happened to him in Cell One, or what happened in the new site, which seemed to me like where they kept people who would later disappear. It would have been so easy for him, my charming brother, to make a sleek drama of his story, but he did not.

IMITATION

Nkem is staring at the bulging, slanted eyes of the Benin mask on the living room mantel as she learns about her husband's girlfriend.

"She's really young. Twenty-one or so," her friend Ijemamaka is saying on the phone. "Her hair is short and curly—you know, those small tight curls. Not a relaxer. A texturizer, I think. I hear young people like texturizers now. I wouldn't tell you *sha*, I know men and their ways, but I heard she has moved into your house. This is what happens when you marry a rich man." Ijemamaka pauses and Nkem hears her suck in her breath—a deliberate, exaggerated sound. "I mean, Obiora is a good man, *of course*," Ijemamaka continues. "But to bring his girlfriend into your house? No respect. She drives his cars all over Lagos. I saw her myself on Awolowo Road driving the Mazda."

"Thank you for telling me," Nkem says. She imagines the way Ijemamaka's mouth scrunches up, like a sucked-until-limp orange, a mouth wearied from talk.

"I had to tell you. What are friends for? What else could I *do*?" Ijemamaka says, and Nkem wonders if it is glee, that highness in Ijemamaka's tone, that inflection in "do."

For the next fifteen minutes, Ijemamaka talks about her visit to Nigeria, how prices have risen since the last time she was back—even *garri* is so expensive now. How so many more children hawk in traffic hold-ups, how erosion has eaten away chunks of the major road to her hometown in Delta State. Nkem clucks and sighs loudly at the appropriate times. She does not remind Ijemamaka that she, too, was back in Nigeria some months ago, at Christmas. She does not tell Ijemamaka that her fingers feel numb, that she wishes Ijemamaka had not called. Finally, before she hangs up, she promises to bring the children up to visit Ijemamaka in New Jersey one of these weekends—a promise she knows she will not keep.

She walks into the kitchen, pours herself a glass of water, and then leaves it on the table, untouched. Back in the living room, she stares at the Benin mask, copper-colored, its abstract features too big. Her neighbors call it "noble"; because of it, the couple two houses down have started collecting African art, and they, too, have settled for good imitations, although they enjoy talking about how impossible it is to find originals.

Nkem imagines the Benin people carving the original masks four hundred years ago. Obiora told her they used the masks at royal ceremonies, placing them on either side of their king to protect him, to ward off evil. Only specially chosen people could be custodians of the mask, the same people who were responsible for bringing the fresh human heads used in burying their king. Nkem imagines the proud young men, muscled, brown skin gleaming with palm kernel oil, graceful loincloths on their waists. She imagines—and this she imagines herself because Obiora did not suggest it happened that way—the proud young men wishing they did not have to behead strangers to bury their king, wishing they could use the masks to protect themselves, too, wishing they had a say.

. . .

She was pregnant when she first came to America with Obiora. The house Obiora rented, and would later buy, smelled fresh, like green tea, and the short driveway was thick with gravel. We live in a lovely suburb near Philadelphia, she told her friends in Lagos on the phone. She sent them pictures of herself and Obiora near the Liberty Bell, proudly scrawled *very important in American history* behind the pictures, and enclosed glossy pamphlets featuring a balding Benjamin Franklin.

Her neighbors on Cherrywood Lane, all white and pale-haired and lean, came over and introduced themselves, asked if she needed help with anything—getting a driver's license, a phone, a maintenance person. She did not mind that her accent, her foreignness, made her seem helpless to them. She liked them and their lives. Lives Obiora often called "plastic." Yet she knew he, too, wanted the children to be like their neighbors', the kind of children who sniffed at food that had fallen on the dirt, saying it was "spoiled." In her life, her childhood, you snatched the food up, whatever it was, and ate it.

Obiora stayed the first few months, so the neighbors didn't start to ask about him until later. Where was her husband? Was something wrong? Nkem said everything was fine. He lived in Nigeria *and* America; they had two homes. She saw the doubt in their eyes, knew they were thinking of other couples with second homes in places like Florida and Montreal, couples who inhabited each home at the same time, together.

Obiora laughed when she told him how curious the neighbors were about them. He said *oyibo* people were like that. If you did something in a different way, they would think you were abnormal, as though their way was the only possible way.

And although Nkem knew many Nigerian couples who lived together, all year, she said nothing.

Nkem runs a hand over the rounded metal of the Benin mask's nose. One of the best imitations, Obiora had said when he bought it a few years ago. He told her how the British had stolen the original masks in the late 1800s during what they called the Punitive Expedition; how the British had a way of using words like "expedition" and "pacification" for killing and stealing. The masks—thousands, Obiora said—were regarded as "war booty" and were now displayed in museums all over the world.

Nkem picks up the mask and presses her face to it; it is cold, heavy, lifeless. Yet when Obiora talks about it—and all the rest—he makes them seem breathing, warm. Last year, when he brought the Nok terra-cotta that sits on the table in the hall-way, he told her the ancient Nok people had used the originals for ancestor worship, placing them in shrines, offering them food morsels. And the British had carted most of those away, too, telling the people (newly Christianized and stupidly blinded, Obiora said) that the sculptures were heathen. We never appreciate what we have, Obiora always ended by saying, before repeating the story of the foolish head of state who had gone to the National Museum in Lagos and forced the curator to give him a four-hundred-year-old bust, which he then gave to the British queen as a present. Sometimes Nkem doubts Obiora's facts, but she listens, because of how passionately he speaks, because of how his eyes glisten as though he is about to cry.

She wonders what he will bring next week; she has come to look forward to the art pieces, touching them, imagining the originals, imagining the lives behind them. Next week, when her children will once again say "Daddy" to someone real, not a telephone voice; when she will wake up at night to hear snoring beside her; when she will see another used towel in the bathroom.

Nkem checks the time on the cable decoder. She has an hour before she has to pick up the children. Through the drapes that her housegirl, Amaechi, has so carefully parted, the sun spills a rectangle of yellow light onto the glass center table. She sits at the edge of the leather sofa and looks around the living room, remembers the delivery man from Ethan Interiors who changed the lampshade the other day. "You got a great house, ma'am," he'd said, with that curious American smile that meant he believed he, too, could have something like it someday. It is one of the things she has come to love about America, the abundance of unreasonable hope.

At first, when she had come to America to have the baby, she had been proudly excited because she had married into the coveted league, the Rich Nigerian Men Who Sent Their Wives to America to Have Their Babies league. Then the house they rented was put up for sale. A good price, Obiora said, before telling her they would buy. She liked it when he said "we," as though she really had a say in it. And she liked that she had become part of yet another league, the Rich Nigerian Men Who Owned Houses in America league.

They never decided that she would stay with the children—Okey was born three years after Adanna. It just happened. She stayed back at first, after Adanna, to take a number of computer courses because Obiora said it was a good idea. Then Obiora registered Adanna in preschool, when Nkem was pregnant with Okey. Then he found a good private elementary school and told her they were lucky it was so close. Only a fifteen-minute drive to take Adanna there. She had never imagined that her children would go to school, sit side by side with white children whose parents owned mansions on lonely hills, never imagined this life. So she said nothing.

Obiora visited almost every month, the first two years, and she and the children went home at Christmas. Then, when he finally got the huge government contract, he decided he would visit only in the summer. For two months. He couldn't travel that often anymore, he didn't want to risk losing those government contracts. They kept coming, too, those contracts. He got listed as one of Fifty Influential Nigerian Businessmen and sent her the photocopied pages from *Newswatch,* and she kept them clipped together in a file.

Nkem sighs, runs her hand through her hair. It feels too thick, too old. She has planned to get a relaxer touch-up tomorrow, have her hair set in a flip that would rest around her neck the way Obiora likes. And she has planned, on Friday, to wax her pubic hair into a thin line, the way Obiora likes. She walks out into the hallway, up the wide stairs, then back downstairs and into the kitchen. She used to walk like this throughout the house in Lagos, every day of the three weeks she and the children spent at Christmas. She would smell Obiora's closet, run her hand over his cologne bottles, and push suspicions from her mind. One Christmas Eve, the phone rang and the caller hung up when Nkem answered. Obiora laughed and said, "Some young prankster." And Nkem told herself that it probably was a young prankster, or better yet, a sincere wrong number.

.   .   .

Nkem walks back upstairs and into the bathroom, smells the pungent Lysol that Amaechi has just used to clean the tiles. She stares at her face in the mirror; her right eye looks smaller than the left. "Mermaid eyes," Obiora calls them. He thinks that mermaids, not angels, are the most beautiful creatures. Her face has always made people talk—how perfectly oval it is, how flawless the dark skin—but Obiora's calling her eyes mermaid eyes used to make her feel newly beautiful, as though the compliment gave her another set of eyes.

She picks up the scissors, the one she uses to cut Adanna's ribbons into neater bits, and raises it to her head. She pulls up clumps of hair and cuts close to the scalp, leaving hair about the length of her thumbnail, just enough to tighten into curls with a texturizer. She watches the hair float down, like brown cotton wisps falling on the white sink. She cuts more. Tufts of hair float down, like scorched wings of moths. She wades in further. More hair falls. Some gets into her eyes and itches. She sneezes. She smells the Pink Oil moisturizer she smoothed on this morning and thinks about the Nigerian woman she met once—Ifeyinwa or Ifeoma, she cannot remember now—at a wedding in Delaware, whose husband lived in Nigeria, too, and who had short hair, although hers was natural, no relaxer or texturizer.

The woman had complained, saying "our men," familiarly, as though Nkem's husband and hers were somehow related to each other. Our men like to keep us here, she had told Nkem. They visit for business and vacations, they leave us and the children with big houses and cars, they get us housegirls from Nigeria who we don't have to pay any outrageous American wages, and they say business is better in Nigeria and all that. But you know why they won't move here, even if business were better here? Because America does not recognize Big

Men. Nobody says "Sir! Sir!" to them in America. Nobody rushes to dust their seats before they sit down.

Nkem had asked the woman if she planned to move back and the woman turned, her eyes round, as though Nkem had just betrayed her. But how can I live in Nigeria again? she said. When you've been here so long, you're not the same, you're not like the people there. How can my children blend in? And Nkem, although she disliked the woman's severely shaved eyebrows, had understood.

Nkem lays the scissors down and calls Amaechi to clean up the hair.

"Madam!" Amaechi screams. "*Chim o!* Why did you cut your hair? What happened?"

"Does something have to happen before I cut my hair? Clean up the hair!"

Nkem walks into her room. She stares at the paisley cover pulled sleek across the king-size bed. Even Amaechi's efficient hands can't hide the flatness on one side of the bed, the fact that it is used only two months of the year. Obiora's mail is in a neat pile on his nightstand, credit card preapprovals, flyers from LensCrafters. The people who matter know he really lives in Nigeria.

She comes out and stands by the bathroom as Amaechi cleans up the hair, reverently brushing the brown strands into a dustpan, as though they are potent. Nkem wishes she had not snapped. The madam/housegirl line has blurred in the years she has had Amaechi. It is what America does to you, she thinks. It forces egalitarianism on you. You have nobody to talk to, really, except for your toddlers, so you turn to your housegirl. And before you know it, she is your friend. Your equal.

"I had a difficult day," Nkem says, after a while. "I'm sorry."

"I know, madam, I see it in your face," Amaechi says, and smiles.

The phone rings and Nkem knows it is Obiora. Nobody else calls this late.

"Darling, *kedu*?" he says. "Sorry, I couldn't call earlier. I just got back from Abuja, the meeting with the minister. My flight was delayed until midnight. It's almost two a.m. now. Can you believe that?"

Nkem makes a sympathetic sound.

"Adanna and Okey *kwanu*?" he asks.

"They are fine. Asleep."

"Are you sick? Are you okay?" he asks. "You sound strange."

"I'm all right." She knows she should tell him about the children's day, she usually does when he calls too late to talk to them. But her tongue feels bloated, too heavy to let the words roll out.

"How was the weather today?" he asks.

"Warming up."

"It better finish warming up before I come," he says, and laughs. "I booked my flight today. I can't wait to see you all."

"Do you—?" she starts to say, but he cuts her off.

"Darling, I have to go. I have a call coming in, it's the minister's personal assistant calling at this time! I love you."

"I love you," she says, although the phone is already dead. She tries to visualize Obiora, but she can't because she is not sure if he is at home, in his car, somewhere else. And then she wonders if he is alone, or if he is with the girl with the short curly hair. Her mind wanders to the bedroom in Nigeria, hers and Obiora's, that still feels like a hotel room every Christmas.

Does this girl clutch her pillow in sleep? Do this girl's moans bounce off the vanity mirror? Does this girl walk to the bathroom on tiptoe as she herself had done as a single girl when her married boyfriend brought her to his house for a wife-away weekend?

She dated married men before Obiora—what single girl in Lagos hadn't? Ikenna, a businessman, had paid her father's hospital bills after the hernia surgery. Tunji, a retired army general, had fixed the roof of her parents' home and bought them the first real sofas they had ever owned. She would have considered being his fourth wife—he was a Muslim and could have proposed—so that he would help her with her younger siblings' education. She was the *ada*, after all, and it shamed her, even more than it frustrated her, that she could not do any of the things expected of the First Daughter, that her parents still struggled on the parched farm, that her siblings still hawked loaves of bread at the motor park. But Tunji did not propose. There were other men after him, men who praised her baby skin, men who gave her fleeting handouts, men who never proposed because she had gone to secretarial school, not a university. Because despite her perfect face she still mixed up her English tenses; because she was still, essentially, a Bush Girl.

Then she met Obiora on a rainy day when he walked into the reception area of the advertising agency and she smiled and said, "Good morning, sir. Can I help you?" And he said, "Yes, please make the rain stop." Mermaid Eyes, he called her that first day. He did not ask her to meet him at a private guest-house, like all the other men, but instead took her to dinner at the vibrantly public Lagoon restaurant, where anybody could have seen them. He asked about her family. He ordered wine that tasted sour on her tongue, telling her, "You will come to like it," and so she made herself like the wine right away. She was nothing like the wives of his friends, the kind of women who went abroad and bumped into each other while shopping at Harrods, and she held her breath waiting for Obiora to realize this and leave her. But the months passed and he had her siblings enrolled in school and he introduced her to his friends at the boat club and he moved her out of the self-contained in Ojota and into a real flat with a balcony in Ikeja. When he asked if she would marry him, she thought how unnecessary it was, his asking, since she would have been happy simply to be told.

Nkem feels a fierce possessiveness now, imagining this girl locked in Obiora's arms, on their bed. She puts the phone down, tells Amaechi she will be right back, and drives to Walgreens to buy a carton of texturizer. Back in the car, she turns the light on and stares at the carton, at the picture of the women with tightly curled hair.

Nkem watches Amaechi slice potatoes, watches the thin skin descend in a translucent brown spiral.

"Be careful. You are peeling it so close," she says.

"My mother used to rub yam peel on my skin if I took away too much yam with the peel. It itched for days," Amaechi says with a short laugh. She is cutting the potatoes into quarters. Back home, she would have used yams for the *ji akwukwo* pottage, but here there are hardly any yams at the African store— real African yams, not the fibrous potatoes the American supermarkets sell as yams. Imitation yams, Nkem thinks, and smiles. She has never told Amaechi how similar their childhoods were. Her mother may not have rubbed yam peels on her skin, but then there were hardly any yams. Instead, there was improvised food. She remembers how her mother plucked plant leaves that nobody else ate and made a soup with them, insisting they were edible. They always tasted, to Nkem, like urine, because she would see the neighborhood boys urinating on the stems of those plants.

"Do you want me to use the spinach or the dried *onugbu*, madam?" Amaechi asks. She always asks, when Nkem sits in as she cooks. Do you want me to use the red onion or the white? Beef broth or chicken?

"Use whichever you like," Nkem says. She does not miss the look Amaechi darts her. Usually Nkem will say use that or use this. Now she wonders why they go through the charade, who they are trying to fool; they both know that Amaechi is much better in the kitchen than she is.

Nkem watches as Amaechi washes the spinach in the sink, the vigor in Amaechi's shoulders, the wide solid hips. She remembers the shy, eager sixteen-year-old Obiora brought to America, who for months remained fascinated by the dishwasher. Obiora had employed Amaechi's father as a driver, bought him his own motorcycle and said Amaechi's parents had embarrassed him, kneeling down on the dirt to thank him, clutching his legs.

Amaechi is shaking the colander full of spinach leaves when Nkem says, "Your *oga* Obiora has a girlfriend who has moved into the house in Lagos."

Amaechi drops the colander into the sink. "Madam?"

"You heard me," Nkem says. She and Amaechi talk about which Rugrats character the children mimic best, how Uncle Ben's is better than basmati for *jollof* rice, how American children talk to elders as if they were their equals. But they have never talked about Obiora except to discuss what he will eat, or how to launder his shirts, when he visits.

"How do you know, madam?" Amaechi asks finally, turning around to look at Nkem.

"My friend Ijemamaka called and told me. She just got back from Nigeria."

Amaechi is staring at Nkem boldly, as though challenging her to take back her words. "But madam—is she sure?"

"I am sure she would not lie to me about something like that," Nkem says, leaning back on her chair. She feels ridiculous. To think that she is affirming that her husband's girlfriend has moved into her home. Perhaps she should doubt it; she should remember Ijemamaka's brittle envy, the way Ijemamaka always has something tear-her-down to say. But none of this matters, because she knows it is true: a stranger is in her home. And it hardly feels right, referring to the house in Lagos, in the Victoria Garden City neighborhood where mansions skulk behind high gates, as home. *This* is home, this brown house in suburban Philadelphia with sprinklers that make perfect water arcs in the summer.

"When *oga* Obiora comes next week, madam, you will discuss it with him," Amaechi says with a resigned air, pouring vegetable oil into a pot. "He will ask her to move out. It is not right, moving her into your house."

"So after he moves her out, then what?"

"You will forgive him, madam. Men are like that."

Nkem watches Amaechi, the way her feet, encased in blue slippers, are so firm, so flatly placed on the ground. "What if I told you that he has a girlfriend? Not that she has moved in, only that he has a girlfriend."

"I don't know, madam." Amaechi avoids Nkem's eyes. She

pours onion slices into the sizzling oil and backs away at the hissing sound.

"You think your *oga* Obiora has always had girlfriends, don't you?"

Amaechi stirs the onions. Nkem senses the quiver in her hands.

"It is not my place, madam."

"I would not have told you if I did not want to talk to you about it, Amaechi."

"But madam, you know, too."

"I know? I know what?"

"You know *oga* Obiora has girlfriends. You don't ask questions. But inside, you know."

Nkem feels an uncomfortable tingle in her left ear. What does it mean to know, really? Is it knowing—her refusal to think concretely about other women? Her refusal to ever consider the possibility?

"*Oga* Obiora is a good man, madam, and he loves you, he does not use you to play football." Amaechi takes the pot off the stove and looks steadily at Nkem. Her voice is softer, almost cajoling. "Many women would be jealous, maybe your friend Ijemamaka is jealous. Maybe she is not a true friend. There are things she should not tell you. There are things that are good if you don't know."

Nkem runs her hand through her short curly hair, sticky with the texturizer and curl activator she had used earlier. Then she gets up to rinse her hand. She wants to agree with Amaechi, that there are things that are best unknown, but then she is not so sure anymore. Maybe it is not such a bad thing that Ijemamaka told me, she thinks. It no longer matters *why* Ijemamaka called.

"Check the potatoes," she says.

.   .   .

Later that evening, after putting the children to bed, she picks up the kitchen phone and dials the fourteen-digit number. She hardly ever calls Nigeria. Obiora does the calling, because his Worldnet cell phone has good international rates.

"Hello? Good evening." It is a male voice. Uneducated. Rural Igbo accent.

"This is Madam from America."

"Ah, madam!" The voice changes, warms up. "Good evening, madam."

"Who is speaking?"

"Uchenna, madam. I am the new houseboy."

"When did you come?"

"Two weeks now, madam."

"Is *Oga* Obiora there?"

"No, madam. Not back from Abuja."

"Is anybody else there?"

"How, madam?"

"Is anybody else there?"

"Sylvester and Maria, madam."

Nkem sighs. She knows the steward and cook would be there, of course, it is midnight in Nigeria. But does this new houseboy sound hesitant, this new houseboy that Obiora forgot to mention to her? Is the girl with the curly hair there? Or did she go with Obiora on the business trip to Abuja?

"Is anybody else there?" Nkem asks again.

A pause. "Madam?"

"Is anybody else in that house except for Sylvester and Maria?"

"No, madam. No."

"Are you sure?"

A longer pause. "Yes, madam."

"Okay, tell *oga* Obiora that I called."

Nkem hangs up quickly. This is what I have become, she thinks. I am spying on my husband with a new houseboy I don't even know.

"Do you want a small drink?" Amaechi asks, watching her, and Nkem wonders if it is pity, that liquid glint in Amaechi's slightly slanted eyes. A small drink has been their tradition, hers and Amaechi's, for some years now, since the day Nkem got her green card. She had opened a bottle of champagne that day and poured for Amaechi and herself, after the children went to bed. "To America!" she'd said, amid Amaechi's too-loud laughter. She would no longer have to apply for visas to get back into America, no longer have to put up with condescending questions at the American embassy. Because of the crisp plastic card sporting the photo in which she looked sulky. Because she really belonged to this country now, this country of curiosities and crudities, this country where you could drive at night and not fear armed robbers, where restaurants served one person enough food for three.

She does miss home, though, her friends, the cadence of Igbo and Yoruba and pidgin English spoken around her. And when the snow covers the yellow fire hydrant on the street, she misses the Lagos sun that glares down even when it rains. She has sometimes thought about moving back home, but never seriously, never concretely. She goes to a Pilates class twice a week in Philadelphia with her neighbor; she bakes cookies for her children's classes and hers are always the favorites; she expects banks to have drive-ins. America has grown on her, snaked its roots under her skin. "Yes, a small drink," she says to Amaechi. "Bring the wine that is in the fridge and two glasses."

. . .

Nkem has not waxed her pubic hair; there is no thin line between her legs as she drives to the airport to pick Obiora up. She looks in the rearview mirror, at Okey and Adanna strapped in the backseat. They are quiet today, as though they sense her reserve, the laughter that is not on her face. She used to laugh often, driving to the airport to pick Obiora up, hugging him, watching him hug the children. They would have dinner out the first day, Chili's or some other restaurant where Obiora would look on as the children colored their menus. Obiora would give out presents when they got home and the children would stay up late, playing with new toys. And she would wear whatever heady new perfume he'd bought her to bed, and one of the lacy nightdresses she wore only two months a year.

He always marveled at what the children could do, what they liked and didn't like, although they were all things she had told him on the phone. When Okey ran to him with a boo-boo, he kissed it, then laughed at the quaint American custom of kissing wounds. Does spit make a wound heal? he would ask. When his friends visited or called, he asked the children to greet Uncle, but first he teased his friends with "I hope you understand the big-big English they speak; they are *Americanah* now, oh!"

At the airport, the children hug Obiora with the same old abandon, shouting, "Daddy!"

Nkem watches them. Soon they will stop being lured by toys and summer trips and start to question a father they see so few times a year.

After Obiora kisses her lips, he moves back to look at her. He looks unchanged: a short, ordinary light-skinned man wearing an expensive sports jacket and a purple shirt. "Darling, how are you?" he asks. "You cut your hair?"

Nkem shrugs, smiles in the way that says *Pay attention to the children first*. Adanna is pulling at Obiora's hand, asking what did Daddy bring and can she open his suitcase in the car.

After dinner, Nkem sits on the bed and examines the Ife bronze head, which Obiora has told her is actually made of brass. It is stained, life-size, turbaned. It is the first original Obiora has brought.

"We'll have to be very careful with this one," he says.

"An original," she says, surprised, running her hand over the parallel incisions on the face.

"Some of them date back to the eleventh century." He sits next to her to take off his shoes. His voice is high, excited. "But this one is eighteenth-century. Amazing. Definitely worth the cost."

"What was it used for?"

"Decoration for the king's palace. Most of them are made to remember or honor the kings. Isn't it perfect?"

"Yes," she says. "I'm sure they did terrible things with this one, too."

"What?"

"Like they did with the Benin masks. You told me they killed people so they could get human heads to bury the king."

Obiora's gaze is steady on her.

She taps the bronze head with a fingernail. "Do you think the people were happy?" she asks.

"What people?"

"The people who had to kill for their king. I'm sure they wished they could change the way things were, they couldn't have been *happy*."

Obiora's head is tilted to the side as he stares at her. "Well, maybe nine hundred years ago they didn't define 'happy' like you do now."

She puts the bronze head down; she wants to ask him how he defines "happy."

"Why did you cut your hair?" Obiora asks.

"Don't you like it?"

"I loved your long hair."

"You don't like short hair?"

"Why did you cut it? Is it the new fashion trend in America?" He laughs, taking his shirt off to get in the shower.

His belly looks different. Rounder and riper. She wonders how girls in their twenties can stand that blatant sign of self-indulgent middle age. She tries to remember the married men she had dated. Had they ripe bellies like Obiora? She can't recall. Suddenly, she can't remember anything, can't remember where her life has gone.

"I thought you would like it," she says.

"Anything will look good with your lovely face, darling, but I liked your long hair better. You should grow it back. Long hair is more graceful on a Big Man's wife." He makes a face when he says "Big Man," and laughs.

He is naked now; he stretches and she watches the way his belly bobs up and down. In the early years, she would shower with him, sink down to her knees and take him in her mouth, excited by him and by the steam enclosing them. But now, things are different. She has softened like his belly, become pliable, accepting. She watches him walk into the bathroom.

"Can we cram a year's worth of marriage into two months in the summer and three weeks in December?" she asks. "Can we compress marriage?"

Obiora flushes the toilet, door open. "What?"

"*Rapuba*. Nothing."

"Shower with me."

She turns the TV on and pretends she has not heard him. She wonders about the girl with the short curly hair, if she showers with Obiora. She tries, but she cannot visualize the shower in the house in Lagos. A lot of gold trimmings—but she might be confusing it with a hotel bathroom.

"Darling? Shower with me," Obiora says, peeking out of the bathroom. He has not asked in a couple of years. She starts to undress.

In the shower, as she soaps his back, she says, "We have to find a school for Adanna and Okey in Lagos." She had not planned to say it, but it seems right, it is what she has always wanted to say.

Obiora turns to stare at her. "What?"

"We are moving back at the end of the school year. We are moving back to live in Lagos. We are moving back." She speaks slowly, to convince him, to convince herself as well. Obiora continues to stare at her and she knows that he has never heard her speak up, never heard her take a stand. She wonders vaguely if that is what attracted him to her in the first place, that she deferred to him, that she let him speak for both of them.

"We can spend holidays here, together," she says. She stresses the "we."

"What . . . ? Why?" Obiora asks.

"I want to know when a new houseboy is hired in my house," Nkem says. "And the children need you."

"If that is what you want," Obiora says finally. "We'll talk about it."

She gently turns him around and continues to soap his back. There is nothing left to talk about, Nkem knows; it is done.

A PRIVATE EXPERIENCE

Chika climbs in through the store window first and then holds the shutter as the woman climbs in after her. The store looks as if it was deserted long before the riots started; the empty rows of wooden shelves are covered in yellow dust, as are the metal containers stacked in a corner. The store is small, smaller than Chika's walk-in closet back home. The woman climbs in and the window shutters squeak as Chika lets go of them. Chika's hands are trembling, her calves burning after the unsteady run from the market in her high-heeled sandals. She wants to thank the woman, for stopping her as she dashed past, for saying "No run that way!" and for leading her, instead, to this empty store where they could hide. But before she can say thank you, the woman says, reaching out to touch her bare neck, "My necklace lost when I'm running."

"I dropped everything," Chika says. "I was buying oranges and I dropped the oranges and my handbag." She does not add that the handbag was a Burberry, an original one that her mother had bought on a recent trip to London.

The woman sighs and Chika imagines that she is thinking of her necklace, probably plastic beads threaded on a piece of string. Even without the woman's strong Hausa accent, Chika can tell she is a Northerner, from the narrowness of her face, the unfamiliar rise of her cheekbones; and that she is Muslim, because of the scarf. It hangs around the woman's neck now, but it was probably wound loosely round her face before, covering her ears. A long, flimsy pink and black scarf, with the garish prettiness of cheap things. Chika wonders if the woman is looking at her as well, if the woman can tell, from her light complexion and the silver finger rosary her mother insists she wear, that she is Igbo and Christian. Later, Chika will learn that, as she and the woman are speaking, Hausa Muslims are hacking down Igbo Christians with machetes, clubbing them with stones. But now she says, "Thank you for calling me. Everything happened so fast and everybody ran and I was suddenly alone and I didn't know what I was doing. Thank you."

"This place safe," the woman says, in a voice that is so soft it sounds like a whisper. "Them not going to small-small shop, only big-big shop and market."

"Yes," Chika says. But she has no reason to agree or disagree, she knows nothing about riots: the closest she has come is the pro-democracy rally at the university a few weeks ago, where she had held a bright green branch and joined in chanting "The military must go! Abacha must go! Democracy now!" Besides, she would not even have participated in that rally if her sister Nnedi had not been one of the organizers who had gone from hostel to hostel to hand out fliers and talk to students about the importance of "having our voices heard."

Chika's hands are still trembling. Just half an hour ago, she was in the market with Nnedi. She was buying oranges and Nnedi had walked farther down to buy groundnuts and then there was shouting in English, in pidgin, in Hausa, in Igbo.

"Riot! Trouble is coming, oh! They have killed a man!" Then people around her were running, pushing against one another, overturning wheelbarrows full of yams, leaving behind bruised vegetables they had just bargained hard for. Chika smelled the sweat and fear and she ran, too, across wide streets, into this narrow one, which she feared—felt—was dangerous, until she saw the woman.

She and the woman stand silently in the store for a while, looking out of the window they have just climbed through, its squeaky wooden shutters swinging in the air. The street is quiet at first, and then they hear the sound of running feet. They both move away from the window, instinctively, although Chika can still see a man and a woman walking past, the woman holding her wrapper up above her knees, a baby tied to her back. The man is speaking swiftly in Igbo and all Chika hears is "She may have run to Uncle's house."

"Close window," the woman says.

Chika shuts the windows and without the air from the street flowing in, the dust in the room is suddenly so thick she can see it, billowing above her. The room is stuffy and smells nothing like the streets outside, which smell like the kind of sky-colored smoke that wafts around during Christmas when people throw goat carcasses into fires to burn the hair off the skin. The streets where she ran blindly, not sure in which direction Nnedi had run, not sure if the man running beside her was a friend or an enemy, not sure if she should stop and pick up one of the bewildered-looking children separated from their mothers in the rush, not even sure who was who or who was killing whom.

Later she will see the hulks of burned cars, jagged holes in place of their windows and windshields, and she will imagine the burning cars dotting the city like picnic bonfires, silent witnesses to so much. She will find out it had all started at the motor park, when a man drove over a copy of the Holy Koran that lay on the roadside, a man who happened to be Igbo and Christian. The men nearby, men who sat around all day playing draughts, men who happened to be Muslim, pulled him out of his pickup truck, cut his head off with one flash of a machete, and carried it to the market, asking others to join in; the infidel had desecrated the Holy Book. Chika will imagine the man's head, his skin ashen in death, and she will throw up and retch until her stomach is sore. But now, she asks the woman, "Can you still smell the smoke?"

"Yes," the woman says. She unties her green wrapper and spreads it on the dusty floor. She has on only a blouse and a shimmery black slip torn at the seams. "Come and sit."

Chika looks at the threadbare wrapper on the floor; it is probably one of the two the woman owns. She looks down at her own denim skirt and red T-shirt embossed with a picture of the Statue of Liberty, both of which she bought when she and Nnedi spent a few summer weeks with relatives in New York. "No, your wrapper will get dirty," she says.

"Sit," the woman says. "We are waiting here long time."

"Do you know how long . . . ?"

"This night or tomorrow morning."

Chika raises her hand to her forehead, as though checking for a malaria fever. The touch of her cool palm usually calms her, but this time her palm is moist and sweaty. "I left my sister buying groundnuts. I don't know where she is."

"She is going safe place."

"Nnedi."

"Eh?"

"My sister. Her name is Nnedi."

"Nnedi," the woman repeats, and her Hausa accent sheaths the Igbo name in a feathery gentleness.

Later, Chika will comb the hospital mortuaries looking for Nnedi; she will go to newspaper offices clutching the photo of herself and Nnedi taken at a wedding just the week before, the one where she has a stupid half smile on her face because Nnedi pinched her just before the photo was taken, the two of them wearing matching off-the-shoulder Ankara gowns. She will tape copies of the photo on the walls of the market and the nearby stores. She will not find Nnedi. She will never find Nnedi. But now she says to the woman, "Nnedi and I came up here last week to visit our aunty. We are on vacation from school."

"Where you go school?" the woman asks.

"We are at the University of Lagos. I am reading medicine. Nnedi is in political science." Chika wonders if the woman even knows what going to university means. And she wonders, too, if she mentioned school only to feed herself the reality she needs now—that Nnedi is not lost in a riot, that Nnedi is safe somewhere, probably laughing in her easy, mouth-all-open way, probably making one of her political arguments. Like how the government of General Abacha was using its foreign policy to legitimize itself in the eyes of other African countries. Or how the huge popularity in blond hair attachments was a direct result of British colonialism.

"We have only spent a week here with our aunty, we have never even been to Kano before," Chika says, and she realizes that what she feels is this: she and her sister should not be affected by the riot. Riots like this were what she read about in newspapers. Riots like this were what happened to other people.

"Your aunty is in market?" the woman asks.

"No, she's at work. She is the director at the secretariat." Chika raises her hand to her forehead again. She lowers herself and sits, much closer to the woman than she ordinarily would have, so as to rest her body entirely on the wrapper. She smells something on the woman, something harsh like the bar soap their housegirl uses to wash the bed linen.

"Your aunty is going safe place."

"Yes," Chika says. The conversation seems surreal; she feels as if she is watching herself. "I still can't believe this is happening, this riot."

The woman is staring straight ahead. Everything about her is long and slender, her legs stretched out in front of her, her fingers with henna-stained nails, her feet. "It is work of evil," she says finally.

Chika wonders if that is all the woman thinks of the riots, if that is all she sees them as—evil. She wishes Nnedi were here. She imagines the cocoa brown of Nnedi's eyes lighting up, her lips moving quickly, explaining that riots do not happen in a vacuum, that religion and ethnicity are often politicized because the ruler is safe if the hungry ruled are killing one another. Then Chika feels a prick of guilt for wondering if this woman's mind is large enough to grasp any of that.

"In school you are seeing sick people now?" the woman asks.

Chika averts her gaze quickly so that the woman will not see the surprise. "My clinicals? Yes, we started last year. We see patients at the Teaching Hospital." She does not add that she often feels attacks of uncertainty, that she slouches at the back of the group of six or seven students, avoiding the senior registrar's eyes, hoping she would not be asked to examine a patient and give her differential diagnosis.

"I am trader," the woman says. "I'm selling onions,"

Chika listens for sarcasm or reproach in the tone, but there is none. The voice is as steady and as low, a woman simply telling what she does.

"I hope they will not destroy market stalls," Chika replies; she does not know what else to say.

"Every time when they are rioting, they break market," the woman says.

Chika wants to ask the woman how many riots she has witnessed but she does not. She has read about the others in the past: Hausa Muslim zealots attacking Igbo Christians, and sometimes Igbo Christians going on murderous missions of revenge. She does not want a conversation of naming names.

"My nipple is burning like pepper," the woman says.

"What?"

"My nipple is burning like pepper."

Before Chika can swallow the bubble of surprise in her throat and say anything, the woman pulls up her blouse and unhooks the front clasp of a worn black bra. She brings out the money, ten- and twenty-naira notes, folded inside her bra, before freeing her full breasts.

"Burning-burning like pepper," she says, cupping her breasts and leaning toward Chika, as though in an offering. Chika shifts. She remembers the pediatrics rotation only a week ago: the senior registrar, Dr. Olunloyo, wanted all the students to feel the stage 4 heart murmur of a little boy, who was watching them with curious eyes. The doctor asked her to go first and she became sweaty, her mind blank, no longer sure where the heart was. She had finally placed a shaky hand on the left side of the boy's nipple, and the *brrr-brrr-brrr* vibration of swishing blood going the wrong way, pulsing against her fingers, made her stutter and say "Sorry, sorry" to the boy, even though he was smiling at her.

The woman's nipples are nothing like that boy's. They are

cracked, taut and dark brown, the areolas lighter-toned. Chika looks carefully at them, reaches out and feels them. "Do you have a baby?" she asks.

"Yes. One year."

"Your nipples are dry, but they don't look infected. After you feed the baby, you have to use some lotion. And while you are feeding, you have to make sure the nipple and also this other part, the areola, fit inside the baby's mouth."

The woman gives Chika a long look. "First time of this. I'm having five children."

"It was the same with my mother. Her nipples cracked when the sixth child came, and she didn't know what caused it, until a friend told her that she had to moisturize," Chika says. She hardly ever lies, but the few times she does, there is always a purpose behind the lie. She wonders what purpose this lie serves, this need to draw on a fictional past similar to the woman's; she and Nnedi are her mother's only children. Besides, her mother always had Dr. Igbokwe, with his British training and affectation, a phone call away.

"What is your mother rubbing on her nipple?" the woman asks.

"Cocoa butter. The cracks healed fast."

"Eh?" The woman watches Chika for a while, as if this disclosure has created a bond. "All right, I get it and use." She plays with her scarf for a moment and then says, "I am looking for my daughter. We go market together this morning. She is selling groundnut near bus stop, because there are many customers. Then riot begin and I am looking up and down market for her."

"The baby?" Chika asks, knowing how stupid she sounds even as she asks.

The woman shakes her head and there is a flash of impatience, even anger, in her eyes. "You have ear problem? You don't hear what I am saying?"

"Sorry," Chika says.

"Baby is at home! This one is first daughter. Halima." The woman starts to cry. She cries quietly, her shoulders heaving up and down, not the kind of loud sobbing that the women Chika knows do, the kind that screams *Hold me and comfort me because I cannot deal with this alone.* The woman's crying is private, as though she is carrying out a necessary ritual that involves no one else.

Later, when Chika will wish that she and Nnedi had not decided to take a taxi to the market just to see a little of the ancient city of Kano outside their aunt's neighborhood, she will wish also that the woman's daughter, Halima, had been sick or tired or lazy that morning, so that she would not have sold groundnuts that day.

The woman wipes her eyes with one end of her blouse. "Allah keep your sister and Halima in safe place," she says. And because Chika is not sure what Muslims say to show agreement—it cannot be "amen"—she simply nods.

The woman has discovered a rusted tap at a corner of the store, near the metal containers. Perhaps where the trader washed his or her hands, she says, telling Chika that the stores on this street were abandoned months ago, after the government declared them illegal structures to be demolished. The woman turns on the tap and they both watch—surprised—as water trickles out. Brownish, and so metallic Chika can smell it already. Still, it runs.

"I wash and pray," the woman says, her voice louder now, and she smiles for the first time to show even-sized teeth, the front ones stained brown. Her dimples sink into her cheeks, deep enough to swallow half a finger, and unusual in a face so lean. The woman clumsily washes her hands and face at the tap, then removes her scarf from her neck and places it down on the floor. Chika looks away. She knows the woman is on her knees, facing Mecca, but she does not look. It is like the woman's tears, a private experience, and she wishes that she could leave the store. Or that she, too, could pray, could believe in a god, see an omniscient presence in the stale air of the store. She cannot remember when her idea of God has not been cloudy, like the reflection from a steamy bathroom mirror, and she cannot remember ever trying to clean the mirror.

She touches the finger rosary that she still wears, sometimes on her pinky or her forefinger, to please her mother. Nnedi no longer wears hers, once saying with that throaty laugh, "Rosaries are really magical potions, and I don't need those, thank you."

Later, the family will offer Masses over and over for Nnedi to be found safe, though never for the repose of Nnedi's soul. And Chika will think about this woman, praying with her head to the dust floor, and she will change her mind about telling her mother that offering Masses is a waste of money, that it is just fund-raising for the church.

When the woman rises, Chika feels strangely energized. More than three hours have passed and she imagines that the riot is quieted, the rioters drifted away. She has to leave, she has to make her way home and make sure Nnedi and her Aunty are fine.

"I must go," Chika says.

Again the look of impatience on the woman's face. "Outside is danger."

"I think they have gone. I can't even smell any more smoke."

The woman says nothing, seats herself back down on the wrapper. Chika watches her for a while, disappointed without knowing why. Maybe she wants a blessing from the woman, something. "How far away is your house?" she asks.

"Far. I'm taking two buses."

"Then I will come back with my aunty's driver and take you home," Chika says.

The woman looks away. Chika walks slowly to the window and opens it. She expects to hear the woman ask her to stop, to come back, not to be rash. But the woman says nothing and Chika feels the quiet eyes on her back as she climbs out of the window.

The streets are silent. The sun is falling, and in the evening dimness Chika looks around, unsure which way to go. She prays that a taxi will appear, by magic, by luck, by God's hand. Then she prays that Nnedi will be inside the taxi, asking her where the hell she has been, they have been so worried about her. Chika has not reached the end of the second street, toward the market, when she sees the body. She almost doesn't see it, walks so close to it that she feels its heat. The body must have been very recently burned. The smell is sickening, of roasted flesh, unlike that of any she has ever smelled.

Later, when Chika and her aunt go searching throughout Kano, a policeman in the front seat of her aunt's air-conditioned car, she will see other bodies, many burned, lying lengthwise along the sides of the street, as though someone carefully pushed them there, straightening them. She will look at only one of the corpses, naked, stiff, facedown, and it will strike her that she cannot tell if the partially burned man is Igbo or Hausa, Christian or Muslim, from looking at that charred flesh. She will listen to BBC radio and hear the accounts of the deaths and the riots—"religious with undertones of ethnic tension" the voice will say. And she will fling the radio to the wall and a fierce red rage will run through her at how it has all been packaged and sanitized and made to fit into so few words, all those bodies. But now, the heat from the burned body is so close to her, so present and warm that she turns and dashes back toward the store. She feels a sharp pain along her lower leg as she runs. She gets to the store and raps on the window, and she keeps rapping until the woman opens it.

Chika sits on the floor and looks closely, in the failing light, at the line of blood crawling down her leg. Her eyes swim restlessly in her head. It looks alien, the blood, as though someone had squirted tomato paste on her.

"Your leg. There is blood," the woman says, a little wearily. She wets one end of her scarf at the tap and cleans the cut on Chika's leg, then ties the wet scarf around it, knotting it at the calf.

"Thank you," Chika says.

"You want toilet?"

"Toilet? No."

"The containers there, we are using for toilet," the woman says. She takes one of the containers to the back of the store, and soon the smell fills Chika's nose, mixes with the smells of dust and metallic water, makes her feel light-headed and queasy. She closes her eyes.

"Sorry, oh! My stomach is bad. Everything happening today," the woman says from behind her. Afterwards, the woman opens the window and places the container outside, then washes her hands at the tap. She comes back and she and Chika sit side by side in silence; after a while they hear raucous chanting in the distance, words Chika cannot make out. The store is almost completely dark when the woman stretches out on the floor, her upper body on the wrapper and the rest of her not.

Later, Chika will read in *The Guardian* that "the reactionary Hausa-speaking Muslims in the North have a history of violence against non-Muslims," and in the middle of her grief, she will stop to remember that she examined the nipples and experienced the gentleness of a woman who is Hausa and Muslim.

Chika hardly sleeps all night. The window is shut tight; the air is stuffy, and the dust, thick and gritty, crawls up her nose. She keeps seeing the blackened corpse floating in a halo by the window, pointing accusingly at her. Finally she hears the woman get up and open the window, letting in the dull blue of early dawn. The woman stands there for a while before climbing out. Chika can hear footsteps, people walking past. She hears the woman call out, voice raised in recognition, followed by rapid Hausa that Chika does not understand.

The woman climbs back into the store. "Danger is finished. It is Abu. He is selling provisions. He is going to see his store. Everywhere policeman with tear gas. Soldier-man is coming. I go now before soldier-man will begin to harass somebody."

Chika stands slowly and stretches; her joints ache. She will walk all the way back to her aunty's home in the gated estate, because there are no taxis on the street, there are only army Jeeps and battered police station wagons. She will find her aunty, wandering from one room to the next with a glass of water in her hand, muttering in Igbo, over and over, "Why did I ask you and Nnedi to visit? Why did my chi deceive me like this?" And Chika will grasp her aunty's shoulders tightly and lead her to a sofa.

Now, Chika unties the scarf from her leg, shakes it as though to shake the bloodstains out, and hands it to the woman. "Thank you."

"Wash your leg well-well. Greet your sister, greet your people," the woman says, tightening her wrapper around her waist.

"Greet your people also. Greet your baby and Halima," Chika says. Later, as she walks home, she will pick up a stone stained the copper of dried blood and hold the ghoulish souvenir to her chest. And she will suspect right then, in a strange flash while clutching the stone, that she will never find Nnedi, that her sister is gone. But now, she turns to the woman and adds, "May I keep your scarf? The bleeding might start again."

The woman looks for a moment as if she does not understand; then she nods. There is perhaps the beginning of future grief on her face, but she smiles a slight, distracted smile before she hands the scarf back to Chika and turns to climb out of the window.

GHOSTS

Today I saw Ikenna Okoro, a man I had long thought was dead. Perhaps I should have bent down, grabbed a handful of sand, and thrown it at him, in the way my people do to make sure a person is not a ghost. But I am a Western-educated man, a retired mathematics professor of seventy-one, and I am supposed to have armed myself with enough science to laugh indulgently at the ways of my people. I did not throw sand at him. I could not have done so even if I had wished to, anyway, since we met on the concrete grounds of the university Bursary.

I was there to ask about my pension, yet again. "Good day, Prof," the dried-up-looking clerk, Ugwuoke, said. "Sorry, the money has not come in."

The other clerk, whose name I have now forgotten, nodded and apologized as well, while chewing on a pink lobe of kola nut. They were used to this. I was used to this. So were the tattered men who were clustered under the flame tree, talking loudly among themselves, gesturing. The education minister has stolen the pension money, one fellow said. Another said that it was the vice chancellor who had deposited the money in high-interest personal accounts. They cursed the vice chancellor: His penis will quench. His children will not have children. He will die of diarrhea. When I walked up to them, they greeted me and shook their heads apologetically about the situation, as if my professor-level pension were somehow more important than their messenger-level or driver-level pensions. They called me Prof, as most people do, as the hawkers sitting next to their trays under the tree did. "Prof! Prof! Come and buy good banana!"

I chatted with Vincent, who had been our driver when I was faculty dean in the eighties. "No pension for three years, Prof," he said. "This is why people retire and die."

"*O joka*," I said, although he, of course, did not need me to tell him how terrible it was.

"How is Nkiru, Prof? I trust she is well in America?" He always asks about our daughter. He often drove my wife, Ebere, and me to visit her at the College of Medicine in Enugu. I remember that when Ebere died, he came with his relatives for *mgbalu* and gave a touching, if rather long, speech about how well Ebere had treated him when he was our driver, how she gave him our daughter's old clothes for his children.

"Nkiru is well," I said.

"Please greet her for me when she calls, Prof."

"I will."

He talked for a while longer, about ours being a country that has not learned to say thank you, about the students in the hostels not paying him on time for mending their shoes. But it was his Adam's apple that held my attention; it bobbed alarmingly, as if just about to pierce the wrinkled skin of his neck and pop out. Vincent is younger than I am, perhaps in his late sixties, but he looks older. He has little hair left. I quite remember his incessant chatter while he drove me to work in those days; I remember, too, that he was fond of reading my newspapers, a practice I did not encourage.

"Prof, won't you buy us banana? Hunger is killing us," one of the men gathered under the flame tree said. He had a familiar face. I think he was my next-door neighbor Professor Ijere's gardener. His tone had a half-teasing, half-serious quality, but I bought groundnuts and a bunch of bananas for them, although what all those men really needed was some moisturizer. Their faces and arms looked like ash. It is almost March, but the harmattan season is still very much here: the dry winds, the crackling static on my clothes, the fine dust on my eyelashes. I applied more lotion than usual today, and Vaseline on my lips, but still the dryness made my palms and face feel tight.

Ebere used to tease me about not moisturizing properly, especially in the harmattan, and sometimes after I had my morning bath, she would slowly rub her Nivea on my arms, my legs, my back. We have to take care of this lovely skin, she would say with that playful laughter of hers. She always said my complexion had been the trait that persuaded her, since I did not have any money like all those other suitors who had trooped to her flat on Elias Avenue in 1961. "Seamless," she called my complexion. I saw nothing especially distinctive in my dark umber tone, but I did come to preen a little with the passing years, with Ebere's massaging hands.

"Thank you, Prof!" the men said, and then began to mock one another about who would do the dividing.

I stood around and listened to their talk. I was aware that they spoke more respectably because I was there: carpentry was not going well, children were ill, more moneylender troubles. They laughed often. Of course they nurse resentment, as they well should, but it has somehow managed to leave their spirits whole. I often wonder whether I would be like them if I did not have money saved from my appointments in the Federal Office of Statistics and if Nkiru did not insist on sending me dollars that I do not need. I doubt it; I would probably have hunched up like a tortoise in its shell and let my dignity be whittled away.

Finally I said goodbye to them and walked toward my car, parked near the whistling pine trees that shield the Faculty of Education from the Bursary. That was when I saw Ikenna Okoro.

He called out to me first. "James? James Nwoye, is it you?" He stood with his mouth open and I could see that his teeth are still complete. I lost one last year. I have refused to have what Nkiru calls "work" done, but I still felt rather sour at Ikenna's full set.

"Ikenna? Ikenna Okoro?" I asked in the tentative way one suggests something that cannot be: the coming to life of a man who died thirty-seven years ago.

"Yes, yes." Ikenna came closer, uncertainly. We shook hands, and then hugged briefly.

We had not been good friends, Ikenna and I; I knew him fairly well in those days only because everyone knew him fairly well. It was he who, when the new vice chancellor, a Nigerian man raised in England, announced that all lecturers must wear ties to class, had defiantly continued to wear his brightly colored tunics. It was he who mounted the podium at the Staff Club and spoke until he was hoarse, about petitioning the government, about supporting better conditions for the nonacademic staff. He was in sociology, and although many of us in the proper sciences thought that the social sciences people were empty vessels who had too much time on their hands and wrote reams of unreadable books, we saw Ikenna differently. We forgave his peremptory style and did not discard his pamphlets and rather admired the erudite asperity with which he blazed through issues; his fearlessness convinced us. He is still a shrunken man with froglike eyes and light skin, which has now become discolored, dotted with brown age spots. One heard of him in those days and then struggled to hide great disappointment upon seeing him, because the depth of his rhetoric somehow demanded good looks. But then, my people say that a famous animal does not always fill the hunter's basket.

"You're alive?" I asked. I was quite shaken. My family and I saw him on the day he died, July 6, 1967, the day we evacuated Nsukka in a hurry, with the sun a strange fiery red in the sky and nearby the *boom-boom-boom* of shelling as the federal soldiers advanced. We were in my Impala. The militia waved us through the campus gates and shouted that we should not worry, that the vandals—as we called the federal soldiers—would be defeated in a matter of days and we could come back. The local villagers, the same ones who would pick through lecturers' dustbins for food after the war, were walking along, hundreds of them, women with boxes on their heads and babies tied to their backs, barefoot children carrying bundles, men dragging bicycles, holding yams. I remember that Ebere was consoling our daughter, Zik, about the doll left behind in our haste, when we saw Ikenna's green Kadett. He was driving the opposite way, back onto campus. I sounded the horn and stopped. "You can't go back!" I called. But he waved and said, "I have to get some manuscripts." Or maybe he said, "I have to get some materials." I thought it rather foolhardy of him to go back in, since the shelling sounded close and our troops would drive the vandals back in a week or two anyway. But I was also full of a sense of our collective invincibility, of the justness of the Biafran cause, and so I did not think much more of it until we heard that Nsukka fell on the very day we evacuated and the campus was occupied. The bearer of the news, a relative of Professor Ezike's, also told us that two lecturers had been killed. One of them had argued with the federal soldiers before he was shot. We did not need to be told this was Ikenna.

Ikenna laughed at my question. "I am, I am alive!" He seemed to find his own response even funnier, because he laughed again. Even his laughter, now that I think of it, seemed discolored, hollow, nothing like the aggressive sound that reverberated all over the Staff Club in those days, as he mocked people who did not agree with him.

"But we saw you," I said. "You remember? That day we evacuated?"

"Yes," he said.

"They said you did not come out."

"I did." He nodded. "I did. I left Biafra the following month."

"You left?" It is incredible that I felt, today, a brief flash of that deep disgust that came when we heard of saboteurs—we called them "sabos"—who betrayed our soldiers, our just cause, our nascent nation, in exchange for a safe passage across to Nigeria, to the salt and meat and cold water that the blockade kept from us.

"No, no, it was not like that, not what you think." Ikenna paused and I noticed that his gray shirt sagged at the shoulders. "I went abroad on a Red Cross plane. I went to Sweden." There was an uncertainty about him, a diffidence that seemed alien, very unlike the man who so easily got people to *act*. I remember how he organized the first rally after Biafra was declared an independent state, all of us crowded at Freedom Square while Ikenna talked and we cheered and shouted, "Happy Independence!"

"You went to Sweden?"

"Yes."

He said nothing else, and I realized that he would not tell me more, that he would not tell me just how he had left the campus alive or how he came to be on that plane; I know of the children airlifted to Gabon later in the war but certainly not of people flown out on Red Cross planes, and so early, too. The silence between us was tense.

"Have you been in Sweden since?" I asked.

"Yes. My whole family was in Orlu when they bombed it. Nobody left, so there was no reason for me to come back." He stopped to let out a harsh sound that was supposed to be laughter but sounded more like a series of coughs. "I was in touch with Dr. Anya for a while. He told me about rebuilding our campus, and I think he said you left for America after the war."

In fact, Ebere and I came back to Nsukka right after the war ended in 1970, but only for a few days. It was too much for us. Our books were in a charred pile in the front garden, under the umbrella tree. The lumps of calcified feces in the bathtub were strewn with pages of my *Mathematical Annals*, used as toilet paper, crusted smears blurring the formulas I had studied and taught. Our piano—Ebere's piano—was gone. My graduation gown, which I had worn to receive my first degree at Ibadan, had been used to wipe something and now lay with ants crawling in and out, busy and oblivious to me watching them. Our photographs were ripped, their frames broken. So we left for America and did not come back until 1976. We were assigned a different house, on Ezenweze Street, and for a long time we avoided driving along Imoke Street, because we did not want to see the old house; we later heard that the new people had cut down the umbrella tree. I told Ikenna all of this, although I said nothing about our time at Berkeley, where my black American friend Chuck Bell had arranged for my teaching appointment. Ikenna was silent for a while, and then he said, "How is your little girl, Zik? She must be a grown woman now."

He had always insisted on paying for Zik's Fanta when we took her to the Staff Club on Family Day, because, he said, she was the prettiest of the children. I suspect it was really because we had named her after our president, and Ikenna was an early Zikist before claiming the movement was too tame and leaving.

"The war took Zik," I said in Igbo. Speaking of death in English has always had, for me, a disquieting finality.

Ikenna breathed deeply, but all he said was *"Ndo,"* nothing more than "Sorry." I was relieved he did not ask how—there are not many hows anyway—and that he did not look inordinately shocked, as if war deaths are ever really accidents.

"We had another child after the war, another daughter," I said.

But Ikenna was talking in a rush. "I did what I could," he said. "I did. I left the International Red Cross. It was full of cowards who could not stand up for human beings. They backed down after that plane was shot down at Eket, as if they did not know it was exactly what Gowon wanted. But the World Council of Churches kept flying in relief through Uli. At night! I was there in Uppsala when they met. It was the biggest operation they had done since the Second World War. I organized the fund-raising. I organized the Biafran rallies all over the European capitals. You heard about the big one at Trafalgar Square? I was at the top of that. I did what I could."

I was not sure that Ikenna was speaking to me. It seemed that he was saying what he had said over and over to many people. I looked toward the flame tree. The men were still clustered there, but I could not tell whether they had finished the bananas and groundnuts. Perhaps it was then that I began to feel submerged in hazy nostalgia, a feeling that still has not left me.

"Chris Okigbo died, not so?" Ikenna asked, and made me focus once again. For a moment, I wondered if he wanted me to deny that, to make Okigbo a ghost-come-back, too. But Okigbo died, our genius, our star, the man whose poetry moved us all, even those of us in the sciences who did not always understand it.

"Yes, the war took Okigbo."

"We lost a colossus in the making."

"True, but at least he was brave enough to fight." As soon as I said that, I was regretful. I had meant it only as a tribute to Chris Okigbo, who could have worked at one of the directorates like the rest of us university people but instead took up a gun to defend Nsukka. I did not want Ikenna to misunderstand my intention, and I wondered whether to apologize. A small dust whirl was building up across the road. The whistling pines above us swayed and the wind whipped dry leaves off the trees farther away. Perhaps because of my discomfort, I began to tell Ikenna about the day Ebere and I drove back to Nsukka after the war ended, about the landscape of ruins, the blown-out roofs, the houses riddled with holes that Ebere said were rather like Swiss cheese. When we got to the road that runs through Aguleri, Biafran soldiers stopped us and shoved a wounded soldier into our car; his blood dripped onto the backseat and, because the upholstery had a tear, soaked deep into the stuffing, mingled with the very insides of our car. A stranger's blood. I was not sure why I chose this particular story to tell Ikenna, but to make it seem worth his while I added that the metallic smell of the soldier's blood reminded me of him, Ikenna, because I had always imagined that the federal soldiers had shot him and left him to die, left his blood to stain the soil.

This is not true; I neither imagined such a thing, nor did that wounded soldier remind me of Ikenna. If he thought my story strange, he did not say so. He nodded and said, "I've heard so many stories, so many."

"How is life in Sweden?" I asked.

He shrugged. "I retired last year. I decided to come back and see." He said "see" as if it meant something more than what one did with one's eyes.

"What about your family?" I asked.

"I never remarried."

"Oh," I said.

"And how is your wife doing? Nnenna, isn't it?" Ikenna asked.

"Ebere."

"Oh, yes, of course, Ebere. Lovely woman."

"Ebere is no longer with us; it has been three years," I said in Igbo. I was surprised to see the tears that glassed Ikenna's eyes. He had forgotten her name and yet, somehow, he was capable of mourning her, or perhaps he was mourning a time immersed in possibilities. Ikenna, I have come to realize, is a man who carries with him the weight of what could have been.

"I'm so sorry," he said. "So sorry."

"It's all right," I said. "She visits."

"What?" he asked with a perplexed look, although he, of course, had heard me.

"She visits. She visits me."

"I see," Ikenna said with that pacifying tone one reserves for the mad.

"I mean, she visited America quite often; our daughter is a doctor there."

"Oh, is that right?" Ikenna asked too brightly. He looked relieved. I don't blame him. We are the educated ones, taught to keep tightly rigid our boundaries of what is considered real. I was like him until Ebere first visited, three weeks after her funeral. Nkiru and her son had just returned to America. I was alone. When I heard the door downstairs close and open and close again, I thought nothing of it. The evening winds always did that. But there was no rustle of leaves outside my bedroom window, no *swish-swish* of the neem and cashew trees. There was *no* wind outside. Yet the door downstairs was opening and closing. In retrospect, I doubt that I was as scared as I should have been. I heard the feet on the stairs, in much the same pattern as Ebere walked, heavier on each third step. I lay still in the darkness of our room. Then I felt my bedcover pulled back, the gently massaging hands on my arms and legs and chest, the soothing creaminess of the lotion, and a pleasant drowsiness overcame me—a drowsiness that I am still unable to fight off whenever she visits. I woke up, as I still do after her visits, with my skin supple and thick with the scent of Nivea.

I often want to tell Nkiru that her mother visits weekly in the harmattan and less often during the rainy season, but if I do, she will finally have reason to come here and bundle me back with her to America and I will be forced to live a life cushioned by so much convenience that it is sterile. A life littered with what we call "opportunities." A life that is not for me. I wonder what would have happened if we had won the war back in 1967. Perhaps we would not be looking overseas for those opportunities, and I would not need to worry about our grandson who does not speak Igbo, who, the last time he visited, did not understand why he was expected to say "Good afternoon" to strangers, because in his world one has to justify simple courtesies. But who can tell? Perhaps nothing would have been different even if we had won.

"How does your daughter like America?" Ikenna asked.

"She is doing very well."

"And you said she is a doctor?"

"Yes." I felt that Ikenna deserved to be told more, or maybe that the tension of my earlier comment had not quite abated, so I said, "She lives in a small town in Connecticut, near Rhode Island. The hospital board had advertised for a doctor, and when she came they took one look at her medical degree from Nigeria and said they did not want a foreigner. But she is American-born—you see, we had her while at Berkeley, I taught there when we went to America after the war—and so they had to let her stay." I chuckled, and hoped Ikenna would laugh along with me. But he did not. He looked toward the men under the flame tree, his expression solemn.

"Ah, yes. At least it's not as bad now as it was for us. Remember what it was like schooling in *oyibo*-land in the late fifties?" he asked.

I nodded to show I remembered, although Ikenna and I could not have had the same experience as students overseas; he is an Oxford man, while I was one of those who got the United Negro College Fund scholarship to study in America.

"The Staff Club is a shell of what it used to be," Ikenna said. "I went there this morning."

"I haven't been there in so long. Even before I retired, it got to the point where I felt too old and out of place there. These greenhorns are inept. Nobody is teaching. Nobody has fresh ideas. It is university politics, politics, politics, while students buy grades with money or their bodies."

"Is that right?"

"Oh, yes. Things have fallen. Senate meetings have become personality-cult battles. It's terrible. Remember Josephat Udeana?"

"The great dancer."

I was taken aback for a moment because it had been so long since I had thought of Josephat as he was, in those days just before the war, by far the best ballroom dancer we had on campus. "Yes, yes, he was," I said, and I felt grateful that Ikenna's memories were frozen at a time when I still thought Josephat to be a man of integrity. "Josephat was vice chancellor for six years and ran this university like his father's chicken coop. Money disappeared and then we would see new cars stamped with the names of foreign foundations that did not exist. Some people went to court, but nothing came of that. He dictated who would be promoted and who would be stagnated. In short, the man acted like a solo university council. This present vice chancellor is following him faithfully. I have not been paid my pension since I retired, you know. I'm just coming from the Bursary now."

"And why isn't anybody doing something about all this? Why?" Ikenna asked, and for the briefest moment the old Ikenna was there, in the voice, the outrage, and I was reminded again that this was an intrepid man. Perhaps he would walk over and pound his fist on a nearby tree.

"Well"—I shrugged—"many of the lecturers are changing their official dates of birth. They go to Personnel Services and bribe somebody and add five years. Nobody wants to retire."

"It is not right. Not right at all."

"It's all over the country, really, not just here." I shook my head in that slow, side-to-side way that my people have perfected when referring to things of this sort, as if to say that the situation is, sadly, ineluctable.

"Yes, standards are falling everwhere. I was just reading about fake drugs in the papers," Ikenna said, and I immediately thought it a rather convenient coincidence, his bringing up fake drugs. Selling expired medicine is the latest plague of our country, and if Ebere had not died the way she did, I might have found this to be a normal segue in the conversation. But I was suspicious. Perhaps Ikenna had heard how Ebere had lain in hospital getting weaker and weaker, how her doctor had been puzzled that she was not recovering after her medication, how I had been distraught, how none of us knew until it was too late that the drugs were useless. Perhaps Ikenna wanted to get me to talk about all this, to exhibit a little more of the lunacy that he had already glimpsed in me.

"Fake drugs are horrible," I said gravely, determined to say nothing else. But I may have been wrong about Ikenna's plot, because he did not pursue the subject. He glanced again at the men under the flame tree and asked me, "So, what do you do these days?" He seemed curious, as if he was wondering just what kind of life I am leading here, alone, on a university campus that is now a withered skin of what it used to be, waiting for a pension that never comes. I smiled and said that I am resting. Is that not what one does on retiring? Do we not call retirement in Igbo "the resting of old age"?

Sometimes I drop by to visit my old friend Professor Maduewe. I take walks across the faded field of Freedom Square, with its border of mango trees. Or along Ikejiani Avenue, where the motorcycles speed past, students perched astride, often coming too close to one another as they avoid the potholes. In the rainy season, when I discover a new gully where the rains have eaten at the land, I feel a flush of accomplishment. I read newspapers. I eat well; my househelp, Harrison, comes five days a week and his *onugbu* soup is unparalleled. I talk to our daughter often, and when my phone goes dead every other week, I hurry to NITEL to bribe somebody to get it repaired. I unearth old, old journals in my dusty, cluttered study. I breathe in deeply the scent of the neem trees that

screen my house from Professor Ijere's—a scent that is supposed to be medicinal, although I am no longer sure what it is
said to cure. I do not go to church; I stopped going after Ebere
first visited, because I was no longer uncertain. It is our diffidence about the afterlife that leads us to religion. So on Sundays I sit on the verandah and watch the vultures stamp on my
roof, and I imagine that they glance down in bemusement.

"Is it a good life, Daddy?" Nkiru has taken to asking lately on
the phone, with that faint, vaguely troubling American accent.
It is not good or bad, I tell her, it is simply mine. And that is
what matters.

Another dust whirl, both of us blinking to protect our eyes,
made me ask Ikenna to come back to my house with me so
that we could sit down and talk properly, but he said he was on
his way to Enugu, and when I asked if he would come by later,
he made a vague motion with his hands that suggested assent. I
know he will not come, though. I will not see him again. I
watched him walk away, this dried nut of a man, and I drove
home thinking of the lives we might have had and the lives we
did have, all of us who went to the Staff Club in those good
days before the war. I drove slowly, because of the motorcyclists
who respect no rules of the road, and because my eyesight is
not as good as it used to be.

I made a minor scratch as I backed my Mercedes out last
week, and so I was careful parking it in the garage. It is twenty-
three-years old but runs quite well. I remember how excited
Nkiru was when it was shipped back from Germany, where I
bought it when I went to receive the Academy of Science
prize. It was the newest model. I did not know this, but her fellow teenagers did, and they all came to peer at the speedome-
ter, to ask permission to touch the paneling on the dashboard.
Now, of course, everyone drives a Mercedes; they buy them

secondhand, rearview mirrors or headlights missing, from Cotonou. Ebere used to mock them, saying our car is old but much better than all those *tuke-tuke* things people are driving with no seat belts. She still has that sense of humor. Sometimes when she visits, she tickles my testicles, her fingers running over them. She knows very well that my prostate medication has deadened things down there, and she does this only to tease me, to laugh her gently jeering laugh. At her burial, when our grandson read his poem, "Keep Laughing, Grandma," I thought the title perfect, and the childish words almost brought me to tears, despite my suspicion that Nkiru wrote most of them.

I looked around the yard as I walked indoors. Harrison does a little gardening, mostly watering in this season. The rose-bushes are just stalks, but at least the hardy cherry bushes are a dusty green. I turned the TV on. It was still raining on the screen, although Dr. Otagbu's son, the bright young man who is reading electronics engineering, came last week to fix it. My satellite channels went off after the last thunderstorm, but I have not yet gone to the satellite office to find somebody to look at it. One can stay some weeks without BBC and CNN anyway, and the programs on NTA are quite good. It was NTA, some days ago, that broadcast an interview with yet another man accused of importing fake drugs—typhoid fever medicine in this case. "My drugs don't kill people," he said, helpfully, facing the camera wide-eyed, as if in an appeal to the masses. "It is only that they will not cure your illness." I turned the TV off because I could no longer bear to see the man's blubbery lips. But I was not offended, not as egregiously as I would have been if Ebere did not visit. I only hoped that he would not be let free to go off once again to China or India or wherever they go to import expired medicine that will not actually kill people, but will only make sure the illness kills them.

I wonder why it never came up, throughout the years after the war, that Ikenna Okoro did not die. True, we did sometimes hear stories of men who had been thought dead and who walked into their compounds months, even years, after January 1970; I can only imagine the quantity of sand thrown on broken men by family members suspended between disbelief and hope. But we hardly talked about the war. When we did, it was with an implacable vagueness, as if what mattered were not that we had crouched in muddy bunkers during air raids after which we buried corpses with bits of pink on their charred skin, not that we had eaten cassava peels and watched our children's bellies swell from malnutrition, but that we had survived. It was a tacit agreement among all of us, the survivors of Biafra. Even Ebere and I, who had debated our first child's name, Zik, for months, agreed very quickly on Nkiruka: what is ahead is better.

I am sitting now in my study, where I marked my students' papers and helped Nkiru with her secondary school mathematics assignments. The armchair leather is worn. The pastel paint above the bookshelves is peeling. The telephone is on my desk, on a fat phone book. Perhaps it will ring and Nkiru will tell me something about our grandson, how well he did in school today, which will make me smile even though I believe American teachers are not circumspect enough and too easily award an A. If it does not ring soon, then I will take a bath and go to bed and, in the still darkness of my room, listen for the sound of doors opening and closing.

ON MONDAY
OF LAST WEEK

Since Monday of last week, Kamara had begun to stand in front of mirrors. She would turn from side to side, examining her lumpy middle and imagining it flat as a book cover, and then she would close her eyes and imagine Tracy caressing it with those paint-stained fingers. She did so now in front of the bathroom mirror after she flushed.

Josh was standing by the door when she came out. Tracy's seven-year-old son. He had his mother's thick, unarched eyebrows, like straight lines drawn above his eyes.

"Pee-pee or a poopy?" he asked in his mock baby voice.

"Pee-pee." She walked into the kitchen, where the gray venetian blinds cast strips of shadow over the counter, where they had been practicing all afternoon for his Read-A-Thon competition. "Have you finished your juiced spinach?" she asked.

"Yes." He was watching her. He knew—he had to know—that the only reason she went into the bathroom each time she handed him the glass of green juice was to give him a chance to pour it away. It had started the first day Josh tasted it, made a face, and said, "Ugh. I hate it."

"Your dad says you'll have to drink it every day before dinner," Kamara had said. "It's only half a glass, it would take a minute to pour it away," she added, and then turned to go to the bathroom. That was all. When she came out the glass was empty, as it was now, placed beside the sink.

"I'll cook your dinner so you will be all set for Zany Brainy when your dad comes back, okay?" she said. American expressions like "all set'"still felt clunky in her mouth, but she used them for Josh.

"Okay," he said.

"Do you want a fish fillet or chicken with your rice pilaf?"

"Chicken."

She opened the refrigerator. The top shelf was stacked with plastic bottles of juiced organic spinach. Cans of herbal tea had filled that space two weeks ago, when Neil was reading *Herbal Drinks for Children,* and before that, it was soy beverages, and before that, protein shakes for growing bones. The juiced spinach would go soon, Kamara knew, because when she arrived this afternoon, the first thing she noticed was that *A Complete Guide to Juicing Vegetables* was no longer on the counter; Neil must have put it in the drawer over the weekend.

Kamara brought out a package of organic chicken strips. "Why don't you lie down for a bit and watch a movie, Josh," she said. He liked to sit in the kitchen and watch her cook, but he looked so tired. The four other Read-A-Thon finalists were probably as tired as he was, their mouths aching from rolling long, unfamiliar words on their tongues, their bodies tense with the thought of the competition tomorrow.

Kamara watched Josh slot in a Rugrats DVD and lie down on the couch, a slight child with olive skin and tangled curls. "Half-caste" was what they had called children like him back in Nigeria, and the word had meant an automatic cool, light-skinned good looks, trips abroad to visit white grandparents. Kamara had always resented the glamour of half-castes. But in America, "half-caste" was a bad word. Kamara learned this when she first called about the babysitting job advertised in the the *Philadelphia City Paper:* generous pay, close to transportation, car not required. Neil had sounded surprised that she was Nigerian.

"You speak such good English," he said, and it annoyed her, his surprise, his assumption that English was somehow his personal property. And because of this, although Tobechi had warned her not to mention her education, she told Neil that she had a master's degree, that she had recently arrived in America to join her husband and wanted to earn a little money babysitting while waiting for her green card application to be processed so that she could get a proper work permit.

"Well, I need somebody who can commit until the end of Josh's school term," Neil said.

"No problem," Kamara said hastily. She really should not have said that she had a master's degree.

"Maybe you could teach Josh a Nigerian language? He already has French lessons two times a week after school. He goes to an advanced program at Temple Beth Hillel, where they have entrance exams for four-year-olds. He's very quiet, very sweet, a great kid, but I'm concerned that there aren't any biracial kids like him at school or in the neighborhood."

"Biracial?" Kamara asked.

Neil's cough was delicate. "My wife is African-American and I'm white, Jewish."

"Oh, he's a half-caste."

There was a pause and Neil's voice came back, thicker. "Please don't say that word."

His tone made Kamara say "Sorry," although she was not

sure what she was apologizing for. The tone, too, made her certain that she had lost her opportunity for the job, and so she was surprised when he gave her the address and asked if they could meet the following day. He was tall and long-jawed. There was a smooth, almost soothing quality to his speech that she supposed came from his being a lawyer. He interviewed her in the kitchen, leaning against the counter, asking about her references and her life in Nigeria, telling her that Josh was being raised to know both his Jewish and African-American backgrounds, all the while smoothing the silver sticker on the phone that said NO TO GUNS. Kamara wondered where the child's mother was. Perhaps Neil had killed her and stuffed her in a trunk; Kamara had spent the past months watching Court TV and had learned how crazy these Americans were. But the longer she listened to Neil talk, the more certain she was that he could not kill an ant. She sensed a fragility in him, a collection of anxieties. He told her that he was worried that Josh was having a hard time with being different from the other children in his school, that Josh might be unhappy, that Josh didn't see enough of him, that Josh was an only child, that Josh would have issues about childhood when he was older, that Josh would be depressed. Halfway through, Kamara wanted to cut him short and ask, "Why are you worrying about things that have not happened?" She didn't, though, because she was not sure she had the job. And when he did offer her the job—after school until six thirty, twelve dollars an hour paid in cash—she still said nothing, because all he seemed to need, desperately need, was her listening and it did not take much to listen.

Neil told her that his method of discipline was reason-based. He would never smack Josh, because he did not believe in abuse as discipline. "If you make Josh see why a particular behavior is wrong, he'll stop it," Neil said.

Smacking is discipline, Kamara wanted to say, and abuse is a different thing. Abuse was the sort of thing Americans she heard about on the news did, putting out cigarettes on their children's skin. But she said what Tobechi had asked her to say: "I feel the same way about smacking. And of course I will use only the discipline method you approve of."

"Josh has a healthy diet," Neil went on. "We do very little high-fructose corn syrup, bleached flour, or trans fat. I'll write it all out for you."

"Okay." She was not sure what the things he had mentioned were.

Before she left, she asked, "What of his mother?"

"Tracy is an artist. She spends a lot of time in the basement for now. She's working on a big thing, a commission. She has a deadline. . . ." His voice trailed off.

"Oh." Kamara looked at him, puzzled, wondering if there was something distinctly American she was supposed to under-stand from what he had said, something to explain why the boy's mother was not there to meet her.

"Josh isn't allowed in the basement for now, so you can't go down there, either. Call me if there are any problems. I have the numbers on the fridge. Tracy doesn't come up until the evenings. Scooters delivers soup and a sandwich to her every day and she's pretty self-sufficient down there." Neil paused. "You have to make sure you don't bother her for anything whatsoever."

"I have not come here to bother anybody," Kamara said, a little coldly, because he suddenly seemed to be speaking to her as people spoke to housegirls back in Nigeria. She should not have allowed Tobechi to persuade her to take this common job of wiping the buttocks of a stranger's child, she should not have listened when he told her that these rich white people on the

Main Line did not know what to do with their money. But even as she walked to the train station nursing her scratched dignity, she knew that she had not really needed to be persuaded. She wanted the job, any job; she wanted a reason to leave the apartment every day.

And now three months had passed. Three months of babysitting Josh. Three months of listening to Neil's worries, of carrying out Neil's anxiety-driven instructions, of developing a pitying affection for Neil. Three months of not seeing Tracy. At first Kamara was curious about this woman with long dreadlocks and skin the color of peanut butter who was barefoot in the wedding photo on the shelf in the den. Kamara wondered if and when Tracy left the basement. Sometimes she heard sounds from down there, a door slamming shut or faint strains of classical music. She wondered whether Tracy ever saw her child. When she tried to get Josh to talk about his mother, he said, "Mommy's very busy with her work. She'll get mad if we bother her," and because he kept his face carefully neutral, she held back from asking him more. She helped him with homework and played cards with him and watched DVDs with him and told him about the crickets she used to catch as a child and basked in the attentive pleasure with which he listened to her. Tracy's existence had become inconsequential, a background reality like the wheezing on the phone line when Kamara called her mother in Nigeria. Until Monday of last week.

That day, Josh was in the bathroom and Kamara was sitting at the kitchen table looking through his homework when she heard a sound behind her. She turned, thinking it was Josh, but Tracy appeared, curvy in leggings and a tight sweater, smiling, squinting, pushing away long dreadlocks from her face with paint-stained fingers. It was a strange moment. Their eyes held and suddenly Kamara wanted to lose weight and wear makeup again. A fellow woman who has the same thing that you have? her friend Chinwe would say if she ever told her. *Tufia!* What kind of foolishness is that? Kamara had been saying this to herself, too, since Monday of last week. She said this even as she stopped eating fried plantains and had her hair braided in the Senegalese place on South Street and began to sift through piles of mascara in the beauty supply store. Saying those words to herself changed nothing, because what had happened in the kitchen that afternoon was a flowering of extravagant hope, because what now propelled her life was the thought that Tracy would come upstairs again.

Kamara put the chicken strips in the oven. Neil added three dollars an hour for the days when he did not come home on time and she cooked Josh's dinner. It amused her, how "cooking dinner" was made to sound like difficult work when it was really a sanitized string of actions: opening cartons and bags and placing things in the oven and microwave. Neil should have seen the kerosene stove she had used back home with its thick gusts of smoke. The oven beeped. She arranged the chicken strips around the small mound of rice on Josh's plate.

"Josh," she called. "Dinner is ready. Would you like frozen yogurt for dessert?"

"Yes." Josh grinned and she thought about the curve of his lips being exactly like that of Tracy's. She hit her toe against the edge of the counter. She had begun to bump into things too often since Monday of last week.

"Are you okay?" Josh asked.

She rubbed her toe. "I'm fine."

"Wait, Kamara," Josh knelt down on the floor and kissed her foot. "There. That'll make it go away."

She looked down at his little head lowered before her, his

hair in helpless curls, and she wanted to hug him very close. "Thank you, Josh."

The phone rang. She knew it was Neil.

"Hi, Kamara. Is everything okay?"

"Everything is fine."

"How's Josh? Is he scared about tomorrow? Is he nervous?"

"He's fine. We just finished the practice."

"Great." A pause. "Can I say a quick hi?"

"He's in the bathroom." Kamara lowered her voice, watching Josh turn off the DVD player in the den.

"Okay. I'll see you soon. I just literally pushed my last client out of the office. We've managed to get her husband to agree to settle out of court and she was starting to linger too much." He laughed shortly.

"Okay then." Kamara was about to put the phone down when she realized that Neil was still there.

"Kamara?"

"Yes?"

"I'm a little concerned about tomorrow. You know, I'm actually not sure how healthy that kind of competition is at his age."

Kamara ran the tap and rinsed away the last streaks of dark green liquid. "He'll be fine."

"I hope going to Zany Brainy takes his mind off the competition for a little while."

"He'll be fine," Kamara repeated.

"Would you like to come to Zany Brainy? I'll drop you off at home afterwards."

Kamara said she would rather go home. She didn't know why she had lied about Josh being in the bathroom; it had slipped out so easily. Before, she would have chatted with Neil and probably gone along with them to Zany Brainy, but she didn't feel like having that get-along relationship with Neil anymore.

She was still holding the phone; it had started to buzz noisily. She touched the PROTECT OUR ANGELS sticker that Neil had recently placed on the cradle, a day after he called, frantic, because he had just seen a photo on the Internet of a child molester who had recently moved to their neighborhood and who looked exactly like the UPS delivery man. *Where is Josh? Where is Josh?* Neil had asked, as if Josh would have been anywhere else but somewhere in the house. Kamara had hung up feeling sorry for him. She had come to understand that American parenting was a juggling of anxieties, and that it came with having too much food: a sated belly gave Americans time to worry that their child might have a rare disease that they had just read about, made them think they had the right to protect their child from disappointment and want and failure. A sated belly gave Americans the luxury of praising themselves for being good parents, as if caring for one's child were the exception rather than the rule. It used to amuse Kamara, watching women on television talk about how much they loved their children, what sacrifices they made for them. Now, it annoyed her. Now that her periods insisted on coming month after month, she resented those manicured women with their effortlessly conceived babies and their breezy expressions like "healthy parenting."

She put the phone down and tugged at the black sticker to see how easily it would come off. When Neil interviewed her for the job, the NO TO GUNS sticker had been silver, and it was the first thing she told Tobechi about, how strange it was to watch Neil smooth it over and over again, as if in a ritual. But Tobechi was not interested in the sticker. He asked her about the house, details she could not possibly know. Was it a colonial? How old was it? And all the while his eyes were shining with watery dreams. "We will live in a house like that one day in Ardmore, too, or another place on the Main Line," he said.

She said nothing, because it was not where they lived that mattered to her, it was what they had become.

They met in university at Nsukka, both of them in their final years, he in engineering and she in chemistry. He was quiet, bookish, smallish, the kind of boy parents said had "bright prospects." But what drew her was the way he looked at her with awed eyes, eyes that made her like herself. After a month, she moved into his room in the Boys' Quarters on a tree-lined avenue of the campus and they went everywhere together, climbing on the same *okada*, Kamara lodged between Tobechi and the motorcyclist. They took bucket baths together in the bathroom with slimy walls, they cooked on his little stove outside, and when his friends began to call him "woman wrapper," he smiled as if they did not know what they were missing. The wedding, which took place shortly after they completed their National Youth Service, was hurried because an uncle, a pastor, had just offered to help Tobechi get an American visa by including his name in a group going for a conference of the Evangelical Faith Mission. America was about hard work, they both knew, and one would make it if one was prepared to work hard. Tobechi would get to America and find a job and work for two years and get a green card and send for her. But two years passed, then four, and she was in Enugu teaching in a secondary school and doing a part-time master's program and attending the christenings of friends' children, while Tobechi was driving a taxi in Philadelphia for a Nigerian man who cheated all his drivers because none of them had papers.

Another year passed. Tobechi could not send as much money as he wanted to because most of it was going into what he called "sorting his papers." Her aunties' whisperings became louder and louder: What is that boy waiting for? If he cannot organize himself and send for his wife, he should let us know, because a woman's time passes quickly! During their telephone conversations, she heard the strain in his voice and she consoled him and longed for him and cried when she was alone until the day finally came: Tobechi called to say that his green card was on the table in front of him and that it was not even green.

Kamara would always remember the air-conditioned staleness of the air when she arrived at the Philadelphia airport. She was still holding her passport, slightly folded on the page that had the visitor's visa with Tobechi's name as sponsor, when she came out at Arrivals and there he was, lighter-skinned, chubby, laughing. It had been six years. They clung to each other. In the car, he told her that he had sorted his papers as a single person and so they would marry again in America and he would file for her green card. He took off his shoes when they got to the apartment and she looked at his toes, dark against the milk-colored linoleum of the kitchen floor, and noticed that they had sprouted hair. She did not remember his toes with hair. She stared at him as he spoke, his Igbo interspersed with English that had an ungainly American accent: "Amah go" for "I will go." He had not spoken like that on the phone. Or had he, and she had not noticed? Was it simply that seeing him was different and that it was the Tobechi of university that she had expected to find? He excavated memories and aired them, rejoiced in them: Do you remember the night we bought *suya* in the rain? She remembered. She remembered that there had been a crackling thunderstorm and the electric bulbs were blinking and they had eaten the soggy grilled meat with raw onions that made their eyes water. She remembered how they had woken up the next morning with onions heavy on their breath. She remembered, too, how their relationship had been filled with an effortless ease. Now, their silences were awkward, but she told herself that things would get better, they had been apart a long time, after all. In bed, she felt nothing except for the rubbery friction of skin against skin and she clearly remembered the way it used to be between them, he silent and gentle and firm, she loud and grasping and writhing. Now, she wondered if it was even the same Tobechi, this person who seemed so eager, so theatrical, and who, most worrying of all, had begun to talk in that false accent that made her want to slap his face. *I wanna fuck you. I'm gonna fuck you.* The first weekend he took her out to see Philadelphia, they walked up and down Old City until she was exhausted and he asked her to sit on a bench while he went and bought her a bottle of water. As he walked back toward her in his slightly baggy jeans and a T-shirt, the tangerine-colored sun behind him, she thought for a moment that he was somebody she did not know at all. He would come home from his new job as a manager at Burger King bearing a little gift: the latest *Essence* magazine, Maltina from the African store, a chocolate bar. On the day they went to a courthouse to exchange vows in front of an impatient-looking woman, he whistled happily as he knotted his tie and she watched him with a kind of desperate sadness, wanting so much to feel his delight. There were emotions she wanted to hold in the palm of her hand that were simply no longer there.

While he was at work, she would pace the apartment and watch TV and eat everything in the fridge, even spoonfuls of margarine after she had finished the bread. Her clothes pinched her waist and armpits, and so she took to walking around with only her *abada* wrapper tied loosely around her and knotted under her arm. She was finally with Tobechi in America, finally with her good man, and the feeling was one of flatness. It was only Chinwe she felt she could really talk to. Chinwe was the friend who had never told her she was foolish to wait for Tobechi, and if she told Chinwe how she did not like her bed but did not want to get up from it in the morning, Chinwe would understand her bewilderment.

She called Chinwe and Chinwe began to cry after the first hello and *kedu*. Another woman was pregnant for Chinwe's husband and he was going to pay her bride price because Chinwe had two daughters and the woman came from a family of many sons. Kamara tried to soothe Chinwe, raged about the useless husband, and then hung up without saying a word about her new life; she could not complain about not having shoes when the person she was talking to had no legs.

With her mother on the phone, she said everything was fine. "We will hear the patter of little feet soon," her mother said, and she said *"Ise!"* to show that she seconded the blessing. And she did: she had taken to closing her eyes while Tobechi was on top of her, willing herself to become pregnant, because if that did not shake her out of her dismay at least it would give her something to care about. Tobechi had brought her contraception pills because he wanted a year of just the both of them, to catch up, to enjoy each other, but she flushed one pill down the toilet each day and wondered how he could not see the grayness that clouded her days, the hard things that had slipped in between them. On Monday of last week, though, he *had* noticed the change in her.

"You're bright today, Kam," he said as he hugged her that evening. He sounded happy that she was bright. She was both thrilled and sorry, for having this knowledge she could not share with him, for suddenly believing again in ways that had nothing to do with him. She could not tell him how Tracy had come upstairs to the kitchen and how surprised she had been because she had given up wondering what kind of mother this was.

"Hi, Kamara," Tracy had said, coming toward her. "I'm Tracy." Her voice was deep and her womanly body was fluid and her sweater and hands were paint-stained.

"Oh, hello," Kamara said, smiling. "Nice to finally meet you, Tracy."

Kamara held out a hand but Tracy came close and touched her chin. "Did you ever wear braces?"

"Braces?"

"Yes."

"No, no."

"You have the most beautiful teeth."

Tracy's hand was still on her chin, slightly tilting her head up, and Kamara felt, first, like an adored little girl, and then like a bride. She smiled again. She was extremely aware of her body, of Tracy's eyes, of the space between them being so small, so very small.

"Have you ever been an artist's model?" Tracy asked.

"No . . . no."

Josh came into the kitchen and rushed to Tracy, his face lit up. "Mommy!" Tracy hugged him and kissed him and ruffled his hair. "Have you finished your work, Mommy?" He clung to her hand.

"Not yet, honey." She seemed to be familiar with the kitchen. Kamara had expected that she would not know where the glasses were kept or how to operate the water filter. "I'm stuck, so I thought I'd come upstairs for a little while." She was smoothing Josh's hair. She turned to Kamara. "It's stuck right here in my throat, you know?"

"Yes," Kamara said, although she did not know. Tracy was looking right into her eyes in a way that made Kamara's tongue feel blubbery.

"Neil says you have a master's degree," Tracy said.

"Yes."

"That's wonderful. I hated college and couldn't wait to grad-uate!" She laughed. Kamara laughed. Josh laughed. Tracy riffled through the mail on the table, picked up one envelope and tore it open and put it back. Kamara and Josh watched her in silence. Then she turned. "Okay, I guess I better get back to work. See you guys later."

"Why don't you show Josh what you're working on?" Kamara asked, because she could not bear the thought of Tracy leaving.

Tracy seemed taken aback by the suggestion for a moment, then she looked down at Josh. "Want to see it, buddy?"

"Yeah!"

In the basement, a wide painting leaned against the wall.

"It's pretty," Josh said. "Right, Kamara?"

It looked like haphazard splashes of bright paint to her. "Yes. It's very nice."

She was more curious about the basement itself, where Tracy practically lived, the slumping couch and cluttered tables and coffee-stained mugs. Tracy was tickling Josh and Josh was laughing. Tracy turned to her. "Sorry it's such a mess in here."

"No, it's fine." She wanted to offer to clean up for Tracy, any-thing to remain here.

"Neil says you've only just moved to the States? I'd love to hear about Nigeria. I was in Ghana a couple of years ago."

"Oh." Kamara sucked in her belly. "Did you like Ghana?"

"Very much. The motherland informs all of my work." Tracy was tickling Josh but her eyes were steady on Kamara. "Are you Yoruba?"

"No. Igbo."

"What does your name mean? Am I saying it right? Ka-mara?"

"Yes. It's a short form of Kamarachizuoroanyi: 'May God's Grace Be Sufficient for Us.' "

"It's beautiful, it's like music. Kamara, Kamara, Kamara."

Kamara imagined Tracy saying that again, this time in her ear, in a whisper. *Kamara, Kamara, Kamara,* she would say while their bodies swayed to the music of the name.

Josh was running with a paintbrush in his hand and Tracy ran after him; they came close to Kamara. Tracy stopped. "Do you like this job, Kamara?"

"Yes." Kamara was surprised. "Josh is a very good boy."

Tracy nodded. She reached out and, again, lightly touched Kamara's face. Her eyes gleamed in the light from the halogen lamps.

"Would you take your clothes off for me?" she asked in a tone as soft as a breath, so soft Kamara was not sure she had heard correctly. "I'd paint you. But it wouldn't look much like you."

Kamara knew that she was no longer breathing as she should. "Oh. I don't know," she said.

"Think about it," Tracy said, before she turned to Josh and told him she had to get back to work.

"Time for your spinach, Josh," Kamara said, in a voice too loud, and went upstairs, wishing she had said something bolder, wishing Tracy would come up again.

Neil had only just begun letting Josh have chocolate sprinkles, after a new book claimed his sugar-free sweetener was carcinogenic, and so Josh was eating his dessert of organic frozen yogurt dotted with chocolate sprinkles when the garage door opened. Neil was wearing a sleek dark suit. He placed his leather bag down on the counter, said hi to Kamara, and then swooped down on Josh. "Hello, bud!"

"Hi, Daddy." Josh kissed him and laughed when Neil nuzzled his neck.

"How did your reading practice with Kamara go?"

"Good."

"Are you nervous, bud? You'll do great, I bet you'll win. But it doesn't matter if you don't because you're still a winner for Daddy. Are you all set for Zany Brainy? It should be fun. Chum the Cheeseball's first visit!"

"Yes." Josh pushed his plate aside and started to look through his schoolbag.

"I'll look at your school stuff later," Neil said.

"I can't find my shoelaces. I took them out in the playground." Josh brought out a piece of paper from his bag. His dirt-encrusted shoelaces were tangled around it and he pulled the laces apart. "Oh, look! Remember the special family Shabbat cards my class was working on, Dad?"

"Is that it?"

"Yes!" Josh held the crayon-colored paper up, moving it this way and that. In his precociously well-formed hand were the words *Kamara, I'm glad we are family. Shabbat shalom.*

"I forgot to give it to you last Friday, Kamara. So I'll have to wait till tomorrow to give it to you, okay?" Josh said, his face solemn.

"Okay, Josh," Kamara said. She was rinsing off his plate for the dishwasher.

Neil took the card from Josh. "You know, Josh," he said, giving the card back, "it's very sweet of you to give this to Kamara, but Kamara is your nanny and your friend, and this was for family."

"Miss Leah said I could."

Neil looked at Kamara, as if seeking support, but Kamara looked away and focused on opening the dishwasher.

"Can we go, Dad?" Josh asked.

"Sure."

Before they left, Kamara said, "Good luck tomorrow, Josh."

Kamara watched them drive off in Neil's Jaguar. Her feet itched to go down the stairs, to knock on Tracy's door and offer something: coffee, a glass of water, a sandwich, herself. In the bathroom, she patted her newly braided hair, touched up her lipgloss and mascara, then started down the stairs that led to the basement. She stopped many times and went back. Finally she rushed down the stairs and knocked on the door. She knocked again and again.

Tracy opened it. "I thought you'd gone," she said, her expression distant. She was wearing a faded T-shirt and paint-streaked jeans and her eyebrows were so thick and straight they looked fake.

"No." Kamara felt awkward. *Why haven't you come up since Monday of last week? Why have your eyes not lit up at seeing me?* "Neil and Josh just left for Zany Brainy. I'm keeping my fingers crossed for Josh tomorrow."

"Yes." There was something in her demeanor that Kamara feared was an irritated impatience.

"I'm sure Josh will win," Kamara said.

"He just might."

Tracy seemed to be moving back, as if about to shut the door.

"Do you need anything?" Kamara asked.

Slowly, Tracy smiled. She moved forward now, closer to Kamara, too close, her face against Kamara's. "You *will* take your clothes off for me," she said.

"Yes." Kamara kept her belly sucked in until Tracy said, "Good. But not today. Today isn't a good day," and disappeared into the room.

Even before Kamara looked at Josh the next afternoon, she knew he hadn't won. He was sitting in front of a plate of cookies, drinking a glass of milk, with Neil standing beside him. A pretty blond woman wearing ill-fitting jeans was looking at the photographs of Josh posted on the fridge.

"Hi, Kamara. We just got back," Neil said. "Josh was fantastic. He really deserved to win. He was clearly the kid who had worked the hardest."

Kamara ruffled Josh's hair. "Hello, Joshy."

"Hi, Kamara," Josh said, and stuffed a cookie into his mouth.

"This is Maren," Neil said. "She's Josh's French teacher."

The woman said hi and shook Kamara's hand and then went into the den. The jeans dug into her crotch and the sides of her face were stained with a too-cheery shade of blusher and she was nothing like Kamara imagined a French teacher would be.

"The Read-A-Thon ate into their lesson time, so I thought they might have the lesson here and Maren was sweet enough to say yes. It's okay, Kamara?" Neil asked.

"Of course." And all of a sudden, she liked Neil again and she liked the way the blinds sliced up the sunlight coming into the kitchen and she liked that the French teacher was here because when the lesson started, she would go down and ask Tracy if it was the right time to take off her clothes. She was wearing a new balconet bra.

"I'm worried," Neil said. "I think I'm consoling him with a sugar overload. He's had two lollipops. Plus we stopped at Baskin-Robbins." Neil was whispering even though Josh could hear. It was the same unnecessarily hushed tone that Neil had used to tell her about the books he'd donated to Josh's pre-K class at Temple Beth Hillel, books that were about Ethiopian Jews, illustrated with pictures of people where skin was the color of burnished earth, but Josh said the teacher had never read the books to the class. Kamara remembered the way Neil had grasped her hand gratefully after she'd said "Josh will be fine," as if all Neil needed was to have somebody say that.

Now, Kamara said, "He'll get over it."

Neil nodded slowly. "I don't know."

She reached out and squeezed Neil's hand. She felt filled with a generosity of spirit.

"Thanks, Kamara." Neil paused. "I better go. I'll be late today. Is it okay if you make dinner?"

"Of course." Kamara smiled again. Perhaps there might be time to go back down to the basement while Josh ate his dinner, perhaps Tracy would ask her to stay and she would call Tobechi and tell him there had been an emergency and she needed to take care of Josh overnight. The door that led to the basement opened. Kamara's excitement brought a dull throbbing to her temples, and the throbbing intensified when Tracy appeared in her leggings and her paint-stained shirt. She hugged and kissed Josh. "Hey, you are my winner, buddy, my special winner."

Kamara was pleased that Tracy did not kiss Neil, that they said "Hi, you" to each other as though they were brother and sister.

"Hey, Kamara," Tracy said, and Kamara told herself that the reason Tracy seemed normal, not absolutely delighted to see her, was that she did not want Neil to know.

Tracy opened the fridge, took an apple, and sighed. "I'm so stuck. So stuck," she said.

"It'll be fine," Neil murmured. And then, raising his voice so that Maren, in the den, would hear, he added, "You haven't met Maren, have you?"

Neil introduced them. Maren extended her hand and Tracy took it.

"Are you wearing contacts?" Tracy asked.

"Contacts? No."

"You have the most unusual eyes. Violet." Tracy was still holding Maren's hand.

"Oh. Thank you!" Maren giggled nervously.

"They really are violet."

"Oh . . . yes, I think so."

"Have you ever been an artist's model?"

"Oh . . . no . . ." More giggles.

"You should think about it," Tracy said.

She raised the apple to her lips and took a slow bite, her gaze never wavering from Maren's face. Neil was watching them with an indulgent smile, and Kamara looked away. She sat down next to Josh and took a cookie from his plate.

JUMPING
MONKEY HILL

The cabins all had thatch roofs. Names like Baboon Lodge and Porcupine Place were hand-painted beside the wooden doors that led out to cobblestone paths, and the windows were left open so that guests woke up to the rustling of the jacaranda leaves and the steady calming crash of the sea's waves. The wicker trays held a selection of fine teas. At midmorning, discreet black maids made the bed, cleaned the elegant bathtub, vacuumed the carpet, and left wildflowers in handcrafted vases. Ujunwa found it odd that the African Writers Workshop was held here, at Jumping Monkey Hill, outside Cape Town. The name itself was incongruous, and the resort had the complacence of the well-fed about it, the kind of place where she imagined affluent foreign tourists would dart around taking pictures of lizards and then return home still mostly unaware that there were more black people than red-capped lizards in South Africa. Later, she would learn that Edward Campbell had chosen the resort; he had spent weekends there when he was a lecturer at the University of Cape Town years ago.

But she didn't know this the afternoon Edward—an old man

in a summer hat who smiled to show two front teeth the color of mildew—picked her up at the airport. He kissed her on both cheeks. He asked if she had had any trouble with her pre-paid ticket in Lagos, if she minded waiting for the Ugandan whose flight would come soon, if she was hungry. He told her that his wife, Isabel, had already picked up most of the other workshop participants and that their friends Simon and Hermione, who had come with them from London as paid staff, were arranging a welcome lunch back at the resort. He and Ujunwa sat down on a bench in Arrivals. He balanced the sign with the Ugandan's name on his shoulder and told her how humid Cape Town was at this time of the year, how pleased he was about the workshop arrangements. He length-ened his words. His accent was what the British called "posh," the kind some rich Nigerians tried to mimic and ended up sounding unintentionally funny. Ujunwa wondered if he was the one who had selected her for the workshop. Probably not; it was the British Council that had made the call for entries and then selected the best.

Edward had moved a little and sat closer to her. He was ask-ing what she did back home in Nigeria. Ujunwa faked a wide yawn and hoped he would stop talking. He repeated his ques-tion and asked whether she had taken leave from her job to attend the workshop. He was watching her intently. He could have been anything from sixty-five to ninety. She could not tell his age from his face; it was pleasant but unformed, as though God, having created him, had slapped him flat against a wall and smeared his features all over his face. She smiled vaguely and said that she had lost her job just before she left Lagos—a job in banking—and so there had been no need to take leave. She yawned again. He seemed keen to know more and she did not want to say more, and so when she looked up and saw the Ugandan walking toward them, she was relieved.

The Ugandan looked sleepy. He was in his early thirties, square-faced and dark-skinned, with uncombed hair that had tightened into kinky balls. He bowed as he shook Edward's hand with both of his and then turned and mumbled a hello to Ujunwa. He sat in the front seat of the Renault. The drive to the resort was long, on roads haphazardly chiseled into steep hills, and Ujunwa worried that Edward was too old to drive so fast. She held her breath until they arrived at the cluster of thatch roofs and manicured paths. A smiling blond woman showed her to her cabin, Zebra Lair, which had a four-poster bed and linen that smelled of lavender. Ujunwa sat on the bed for a moment and then got up to unpack, looking out of the window from time to time to search the canopy of trees for lurking monkeys.

There were none, unfortunately, Edward told the participants later, as they ate lunch under pink umbrellas on the terrace, their tables pushed close to the railing so that they could look down at the turquoise sea. He pointed at each person and did the introductions. The white South African woman was from Durban, while the black man came from Johannesburg. The Tanzanian man came from Arusha, the Ugandan man from Entebbe, the Zimbabwean woman from Bulawayo, the Kenyan man from Nairobi, and the Senegalese woman, the youngest at twenty-three, had flown in from Paris, where she attended university.

Edward introduced Ujunwa last: "Ujunwa Ogundu is our Nigerian participant and she lives in Lagos." Ujunwa looked around the table and wondered with whom she would get along. The Senegalese woman was the most promising, with the irreverent sparkle in her eyes and the Francophone accent and the streaks of silver in her fat dreadlocks. The Zimbabwean woman had longer, thinner dreadlocks, and the cowries in them clinked as she moved her head from side to side. She seemed hyper, overactive, and Ujunwa thought she might like her, but only the way she liked alcohol—in small amounts. The Kenyan and the Tanzanian looked ordinary, almost indistinguishable—tall men with wide foreheads who were wearing tattered beards and short-sleeved patterned shirts. She thought she would like them in the uninvested way that one likes nonthreatening people. She wasn't sure about the South Africans: the white woman had a too-earnest face, humorless and free of makeup, and the black man looked patiently pious, like a Jehovah's Witness who went from door to door and smiled when each was shut in his face. As for the Ugandan, Ujunwa had disliked him from the airport, and did so even more now because of his toadying answers to Edward's questions, the way he leaned forward to speak only to Edward and ignored the other participants. They, in turn, said little to him. They all knew he was the winner of the last Lipton African Writers' Prize, with an award of fifteen thousand pounds. They didn't include him in the polite talk about their flights.

After they ate the creamy chicken prettied with herbs, after they drank the sparkling water that came in glossy bottles, Edward stood up to give the welcoming address. He squinted as he spoke, and his thin hair fluttered in the breeze that smelled of the sea. He started by telling them what they already knew—that the workshop would be for two weeks; that it was his idea but of course funded graciously by the Chamberlain Arts Foundation, just as the Lipton African Writers' Prize had been his idea and funded also by the good people at the foundation; that they were all expected to produce one story for possible publication in the *Oratory;* that laptops would be provided in the cabins; that they would write during the first week and review each participant's work during the second week; and that the Ugandan would be workshop leader. Then he talked about himself, how African literature had been his cause for forty years, a lifelong passion that started at Oxford. He glanced often at the Ugandan. The Ugandan nodded eagerly to acknowledge each glance. Finally Edward introduced his wife, Isabel, although they had all met her. He told them she was an animal rights activist, an old Africa hand who had spent her teenage years in Botswana. He looked proud when she stood up, as if her tall and lean gracefulness made up for what he lacked in appearance. Her hair was a muted red, cut so that wisps framed her face. She patted it as she said, "Edward, really, an introduction." Ujunwa imagined, though, that Isabel had wanted that introduction, that perhaps she had even reminded Edward of it, saying, Now, dear, remember to introduce me properly at lunch. Her tone would have been delicate.

The next day at breakfast, Isabel used just such a tone when she sat next to Ujunwa and said that surely, with that exquisite bone structure, Ujunwa had to come from Nigerian royal stock. The first thing that came to Ujunwa's mind was to ask if Isabel ever needed royal blood to explain the good looks of friends back in London. She did not ask that but instead said—because she could not resist—that she was indeed a princess and came from an ancient lineage and that one of her forebears had captured a Portuguese trader in the seventeenth century and kept him, pampered and oiled, in a royal cage. She stopped to sip her cranberry juice and smile into her glass. Isabel said, brightly, that she could always spot royal blood and she hoped Ujunwa would support her antipoaching campaign and it was just horrible, horrible, how many endangered apes people were killing and they didn't even eat them, never mind all that talk about bush meat, they just used the private parts for charms.

After breakfast, Ujunwa called her mother and told her about the resort and about Isabel and was pleased when her mother chuckled. She hung up and sat in front of her laptop and thought about how long it had been since her mother had really laughed. She sat there for a long time, moving the mouse from side to side, trying to decide whether to name her character something common, like Chioma, or something exotic, like Ibari.

Chioma lives with her mother in Lagos. She has a degree in economics from Nsukka, has recently finished her National Youth Service, and every Thursday she buys *The Guardian* and scours the employment section and sends out her CV in brown manila envelopes. She hears nothing for weeks. Finally she gets a phone call inviting her to an interview. After the first few questions, the man says he will hire her and then walks across and stands behind her and reaches over her shoulders to squeeze her breasts. She hisses, "Stupid man! You cannot respect yourself!" and leaves. Weeks of silence follow. She helps out at her mother's boutique. She sends out more envelopes. At the next interview, the woman, speaking in the fakest, silliest accent Chioma has ever heard, tells her she wants somebody foreign-educated, and Chioma almost laughs as she leaves. More weeks of silence. Chioma has not seen her father in months, but she decides to go to his new office in Victoria Island to ask if he can help her find a job. Their meeting is tense. "Why have you not come since, eh?" he asks, pretending to be angry, because she knows it is eas-

ier for him to be angry, it is easier to be angry with people after you have hurt them. He makes some calls. He
gives her a thin roll of two-hundred-naira notes. He does
not ask about her mother. She notices that the Yellow
Woman's photo is on his desk. Her mother had described
her well: "She is very fair, she looks mixed, and the thing
is that she is not even pretty, she has a face like an overripe
yellow pawpaw."

The chandelier in the main dining room of Jumping Monkey
Hill hung so low that Ujunwa could extend her hand and
touch it. Edward sat at one end of the long, white-covered
table, Isabel at the other, and the participants in between. The
hardwood floors thumped noisily as waiters walked around
and handed out menus. Ostrich medallions. Smoked salmon.
Chicken in orange sauce. Edward urged everyone to eat the
ostrich. It was simply *mah*-ve-lous. Ujunwa did not like the
idea of eating an ostrich, did not even know that people ate
ostriches, and when she said so, Edward laughed good-
naturedly and said that of course ostrich was an African staple.
Everyone else ordered the ostrich, and when Ujunwa's
chicken, too citrusy, came, she wondered if perhaps she should
have had the ostrich. It looked like beef, anyway. She drank
more alcohol than she had ever drunk in her life, two glasses of
wine, and she felt mellowed and chatted with the Senegalese
about the best ways to care for natural black hair: no silicone
products, lots of shea butter, combing only when wet. She
overheard snatches as Edward talked about wine: Chardonnay
was horribly boring.

Afterwards, the participants gathered in the gazebo—except
for the Ugandan, who sat away with Edward and Isabel. They

slapped at flying insects and drank wine and laughed and teased one another: You Kenyans are too submissive! You Nigerians are too aggressive! You Tanzanians have no fashion sense! You Senegalese are too brainwashed by the French! They talked about the war in the Sudan, about the decline of the African Writers Series, about books and writers. They agreed that Dambudzo Marechera was astonishing, that Alan Paton was patronizing, that Isak Dinesen was unforgivable. The Kenyan put on a generic European accent and, between drags at his cigarette, recited what Isak Dinesen had said about all Kikuyu children becoming mentally retarded at the age of nine. They laughed. The Zimbabwean said Achebe was boring and did nothing with style, and the Kenyan said that was a sacrilege and snatched at the Zimbabwean's wineglass, until she recanted, laughing, saying of course Achebe was sublime. The Senegalese said she nearly vomited when a professor at the Sorbonne told her that Conrad was really on *her side,* as if she could not decide for herself who was on her side. Ujunwa began to jump up and down, babbling nonsense to mimic Conrad's Africans, feeling the sweet lightness of wine in her head. The Zimbabwean staggered and fell into the water fountain and climbed out spluttering, her dreadlocks wet, saying she had felt some fish wriggling around in there. The Kenyan said he would use that for his story—fish in the fancy resort fountain—since he really had no idea what he was going to write about. The Senegalese said her story was really *her* story, about how she mourned her girlfriend and how her grieving had emboldened her to come out to her parents although they now treated her being a lesbian as a mild joke and continued to speak of the families of suitable young men. The black South African looked alarmed when he heard "lesbian." He got up and walked away. The Kenyan said the black South African reminded him of his father, who attended a Holy Spirit Revival church and didn't speak to people on the street because they were not saved. The Zimbabwean, Tanzanian, white South African, and Senegalese all spoke about their fathers.

They looked at Ujunwa and she realized that she was the only one who had said nothing, and for a moment the wine no longer fogged her mind. She shrugged and mumbled that there was really little to say about her father. He was a normal person. "Is he in your life?" the Senegalese asked, with the soft tone that meant she assumed he was not, and for the first time her Francophone accent irritated Ujunwa. "He is in my life," Ujunwa said with a quiet force. "He was the one who bought me books when I was a child and the one who read my early poems and stories." She paused, and everyone was looking at her and she added, "He did something that surprised me. It hurt me, too, but mostly it surprised me." The Senegalese looked as if she wanted to ask more but changed her mind and said she wanted more wine. "Are you writing about your father?" the Kenyan asked and Ujunwa answered with an emphatic NO because she had never believed in fiction as therapy. The Tanzanian told her that all fiction was therapy, some sort of therapy, no matter what anybody said.

That evening, Ujunwa tried to write, but her eyeballs were swimming and her head was aching and so she went to bed. After breakfast, she sat before the laptop and cradled a cup of tea.

Chioma gets a call from Merchant Trust bank, one of the places her father contacted. He knows the chairman of the board. She is hopeful; all the bank people she knows drive nice secondhand Jettas and have nice flats in Gbagada. The deputy manager interviews her. He is dark and good-looking and his glasses have an elegant designer logo on the frames and, as he speaks to her, she desperately wishes he would notice her. He doesn't. He tells her that they would like to hire her to do marketing, which will mean going out and bringing in new accounts. She will be working with Yinka. If she can bring in ten million naira during her trial period, she will be guaranteed a permanent position. She nods as he speaks. She is used to men's attention and is sulky that he does not look at her as a man looks at a woman, and she does not quite understand what he means by going out to get new accounts until she starts the job two weeks later. A uniformed driver takes her and Yinka in an air-conditioned official Jeep—she runs her hand over the smooth leather seat, is reluctant to climb out—to the home of an alhaji in Ikoyi. The alhaji is avuncular and expansive with his smile, his hand gestures, his laughter. Yinka has already come to see him a few times before and he hugs her and says something that makes her laugh. He looks at Chioma. "This one is too fine," he says. A steward serves frosted glasses of chapman. The alhaji speaks to Yinka but looks often at Chioma. Then he asks Yinka to come closer and explain the high-interest savings accounts to him and then he asks her to sit on his lap and doesn't she think he's strong enough to carry her? Yinka says of course he is and sits on his lap, smiling a serene smile. Yinka is small and fair; she reminds Chioma of the Yellow Woman.

What Chioma knows of the Yellow Woman is what her mother told her. One slow afternoon, the Yellow Woman had walked into her mother's boutique on Adeniran Ogunsanya Street. Her mother knew who the Yellow

Woman was, knew the relationship with her husband had been on for a year, knew that he had paid for the Yellow Woman's Honda Accord and her flat in Ilupeju. But what drove her mother crazy was the insult of this: the Yellow Woman coming to her boutique, looking at shoes and planning to pay for them with money that really belonged to her husband. So her mother yanked at the Yellow Woman's weave-on that hung to her back and screamed "Husband snatcher!" and the salesgirls joined in, slapping and beating the Yellow Woman until she ran out to her car. When Chioma's father heard of it, he shouted at her mother and said she had acted like one of those wild women from the street, had disgraced him, herself, and an innocent woman for nothing. Then he left the house. Chioma came back from National Youth Service and noticed that her father's wardrobe was empty. Aunty Elohor, Aunty Rose, and Aunty Uche had all come and said to her mother, "We are prepared to go with you and beg him to come back home or we will go and beg on your behalf." Chioma's mother said, "Never, not in this world. I am not going to beg him. It is enough." Aunty Funmi came and said the Yellow Woman had tied him up with medicine and she knew a good *babalawo* who could untie him. Chioma's mother said, "No, I am not going." Her boutique was failing, because Chioma's father had always helped her import shoes from Dubai. So she lowered prices, advertised in *Joy* and *City People,* and started stocking shoes made in Aba. Chioma is wearing a pair of those shoes the morning she sits in the alhaji's sitting room and watches Yinka, perched on the expansive lap, talking about the benefits of a savings account with Merchant Trust Bank.

. . .

At first, Ujunwa tried not to notice that Edward often stared at her body, that his eyes were never on her face but always lower. The workshop days had taken on a routine of breakfast at eight and lunch at one and dinner at six in the grand dining room. On the sixth day, a blisteringly hot day, Edward handed out copies of the first story to be reviewed, written by the Zimbabwean. The participants were all seated on the terrace, and after he handed out the papers, Ujunwa saw that all the seats under the umbrellas were occupied.

"I don't mind sitting in the sun," she said, already getting up. "Would you like me to stand up for you, Edward?"

"I'd rather like you to lie down for me," he said. The moment was humid, thick; a bird cawed from far away. Edward was grinning. Only the Ugandan and the Tanzanian had heard him. Then the Ugandan laughed. And Ujunwa laughed, because it was funny and witty, she told herself, when you really thought about it. After lunch, she took a walk with the Zimbabwean and as they stopped to pick up shells by the sea, Ujunwa wanted to tell her what Edward had said. But the Zimbabwean seemed distracted, less chatty than usual; she was probably anxious about her story. Ujunwa read it that evening. She thought the writing had too many flourishes, but she liked the story and wrote appreciations and careful suggestions in the margins. It was familiar and funny, about a Harare secondary schoolteacher whose Pentecostal minister tells him that he and his wife will not have a child until they get a confession from the witches who have tied up his wife's womb. They become convinced that the witches are their next-door neighbors, and every morning they pray loudly, throwing verbal Holy Ghost bombs over the fence.

After the Zimbabwean read an excerpt the next day, there was a short silence around the dining table. Then the Ugandan spoke and said there was much energy in the prose. The white South African nodded enthusiastically. The Kenyan disagreed. Some of the sentences tried so hard to be literary that they didn't make sense, he said, and he read one such sentence. The Tanzanian man said a story had to be looked at as a whole and not in parts. Yes, the Kenyan agreed, but each part had to make sense in order to form a whole that made sense. Then Edward spoke. The writing was certainly ambitious, but the story itself begged the question "So what?" There was something terribly passé about it when one considered all the other things happening in Zimbabwe under the horrible Mugabe. Ujunwa stared at Edward. What did he mean by "passé"? How could a story so true be passé? But she did not ask what Edward meant and the Kenyan did not ask and the Ugandan did not ask and all the Zimbabwean did was shove her dreadlocks away from her face, cowries clinking. Everyone else remained silent. Soon they all began to yawn and say good night and walk to their cabins.

The next day, they did not talk about the previous evening. They talked about how fluffy the scrambled eggs were and how eerie the jacaranda leaves that rustled against their windows at night were. After dinner, the Senegalese read from her story. It was a windy night and they shut the door to keep out the sound of the whirling trees. The smoke from Edward's pipe hung over the room. The Senegalese read two pages of a funeral scene, stopping often to sip some water, her accent thickening as she became more emotional, each *t* sounding like a *z*. Afterwards, everyone turned to Edward, even the Ugandan, who seemed to have forgotten that he was workshop leader. Edward chewed at his pipe thoughtfully before he said that homosexual stories of this sort weren't reflective of Africa, really.

"Which Africa?" Ujunwa blurted out.

The black South African shifted on his seat. Edward chewed further at his pipe. Then he looked at Ujunwa in the way one would look at a child who refused to keep still in church and said that he wasn't speaking as an Oxford-trained Africanist, but as one who was keen on the real Africa and not the imposing of Western ideas on African venues. The Zimbabwean and Tanzanian and white South African began to shake their heads as Edward was speaking.

"This may indeed be the year 2000, but how African is it for a person to tell her family that she is homosexual?" Edward asked.

The Senegalese burst out in incomprehensible French and then, a minute of fluid speech later, said, "*I* am Senegalese! *I* am Senegalese!" Edward responded in equally swift French and then said in English, with a soft smile, "I think she had too much of that excellent Bordeaux," and some of the participants chuckled.

Ujunwa was the first to leave. She was close to her cabin when she heard somebody call her and she stopped. It was the Kenyan. The Zimbabwean and the white South African were with him. "Let's go to the bar," the Kenyan said. She wondered where the Senegalese was. In the bar, she drank a glass of wine and listened to them talk about how the other guests at Jumping Monkey Hill—all of whom were white—looked at the participants suspiciously. The Kenyan said a youngish couple had stopped and stepped back a little as he approached them on the path from the swimming pool the day before. The white South African said she got suspicious looks, too, perhaps because she wore only kente-print caftans. Sitting there, staring out into the black night, listening to the drink-softened voices around her, Ujunwa felt a self-loathing burst open in the bottom of her stomach. She should not have laughed when Edward said "I'd rather like you to lie down for me." It had not been funny. It had not been funny at all. She had hated it, hated the grin on his face and the glimpse of greenish teeth and the way he always looked at her chest rather than her face, the way his eyes climbed all over her, and yet she had made herself laugh like a deranged hyena. She put down her half-finished glass of wine and said, "Edward is always looking at my body." The Kenyan and the white South African and Zimbabwean stared at her. Ujunwa repeated, "Edward is always looking at my body." The Kenyan said it was clear from the first day that the man would be climbing on top of that flat stick of a wife and wishing it were Ujunwa; the Zimbabwean said Edward's eyes were always leering when he looked at Ujunwa; the white South African said Edward would never look at a white woman like that because what he felt for Ujunwa was a fancy without respect.

"You all noticed?" Ujunwa asked them. "You all noticed?" She felt strangely betrayed. She got up and went to her cabin. She called her mother, but the metallic voice kept saying "The number you are calling is not available at the moment, please try later," and so she hung up. She could not write. She lay in bed and stayed awake for so long that when she finally fell asleep, it was dawn.

That evening, the Tanzanian read an excerpt of his story about the killings in the Congo, from the point of view of a militiaman, a man full of prurient violence. Edward said it would be the lead story in the *Oratory*, that it was urgent and relevant, that it brought news. Ujunwa thought it read like a piece from *The Economist* with cartoon characters painted in.

But she didn't say that. She went back to her cabin and, although she had a stomachache, she turned on her laptop.

As Chioma sits and stares at Yinka, settled on the alhaji's lap, she feels as if she is acting a play. She wrote plays in secondary school. Her class staged one during the school's anniversary celebration and, at the end, there was a standing ovation and the principal said, "Chioma is our future star!" Her father was there, sitting next to her mother, clapping and smiling. But when she said she wanted to study literature in university, he told her it was not viable. His word, "viable." He said she had to study something else and could always write on the side. The alhaji is lightly running a finger over Yinka's arm and saying, "But you know Savanna Union Bank sent people to me last week." Yinka is still smiling and Chioma wonders whether her cheeks are aching. She thinks about the stories in a metal box under her bed. Her father read them all and sometimes he wrote in the margins: *Excellent! Cliché! Very good! Unclear!* It was he who had bought novels for her; her mother thought novels a waste of time and felt that all Chioma needed were her textbooks.

Yinka says, "Chioma!" and she looks up. The alhaji is talking to her. He looks almost shy and his eyes do not meet hers. There is a tentativeness toward her that he does not show toward Yinka. "I am saying you are too fine. Why is it that a Big Man has not married you?" Chioma smiles and says nothing. The alhaji says, "I have agreed that I will do business with Merchant Trust but you will be my personal contact." Chioma is uncertain what to say.

"Of course," Yinka says. "She will be your contact. We will take care of you. Ah, thank you, sir!"

The alhaji gets up and says, "Come, come, I have some nice perfumes from my last trip to London. Let me give you something to take home." He starts to walk inside and then turns. "Come, come, you two." Yinka follows. Chioma gets up. The alhaji turns again toward her, to wait for her to follow. But she does not follow. She turns to the door and opens it and walks out into the bright sunlight and past the Jeep in which the driver is sitting with the door hanging open, listening to the radio. "Aunty? Aunty, something happen?" he calls. She does not answer. She walks and walks, past the high gates and out to the street where she gets in a taxi and goes to the office to clear out her almost-empty desk.

Ujunwa woke up to the crashing sound of the sea, to a nervous clutch in her belly. She did not want to read her story tonight. She did not want to go to breakfast, either, but she went anyway and said a general good morning with a general smile. She sat next to the Kenyan and he leaned toward her and whispered that Edward had just told the Senegalese that he had dreamed of her naked navel. Naked navel. Ujunwa watched the Senegalese, delicately raising her teacup to her lips, sanguine, looking out at the sea. Ujunwa envied her confident calm. She felt upset, too, to hear that Edward was making suggestive remarks to someone else, and she wondered what her pique meant. Had she come to see his ogling as her due? She was uncomfortable thinking about this, about reading that night, and so in the afternoon, lingering over lunch, she asked the Senegalese what she had said when Edward spoke of her naked navel.

The Senegalese shrugged and said no matter how many dreams the old man had, she would still remain a happy lesbian and there was no need to say anything to him.

"But why do we say nothing?" Ujunwa asked. She raised her voice and looked at the others. "Why do we always say nothing?"

They looked at one another. The Kenyan told the waiter that the water was getting warm and could he please get some more ice. The Tanzanian asked the waiter where in Malawi he was from. The Kenyan asked him if the cooks, too, were from Malawi as all the waiters seemed to be. Then the Zimbabwean said she did not care where the cooks were from because the food at Jumping Monkey Hill was simply sickening, all that meat and cream. Other words tumbled out and Ujunwa was not sure who said what. Imagine an African gathering with no rice and why should beer be banned at the dinner table just because Edward thought wine was proper and breakfast at eight was too early, never mind that Edward said it was the "right" time and the smell of his pipe was nauseating and he had to decide which he liked to smoke, anyway, and stop rolling cigarettes halfway through a pipe.

Only the black South African remained silent. He looked bereft, hands clasped in his lap, before he said that Edward was just an old man who meant no harm. Ujunwa shouted at him, "This kind of attitude is why they could kill you and herd you into townships and require passes from you before you could walk on your own land!" Then she stopped herself and apologized. She should not have said that. She had not meant to raise her voice. The Black South African shrugged, as if he understood that the devil would always do his work. The Kenyan was watching Ujunwa. He told her, in a low voice, that she was angry about more than just Edward and she looked away and wondered if "angry" was the right word.

Later, she went to the souvenir shop with the Kenyan and the Senegalese and the Tanzanian and tried on jewelry made of faux ivory. They teased the Tanzanian about his interest in jewelry—perhaps *he* was gay, too? He laughed and said his possibilities were limitless. Then he said, more seriously, that Edward was connected and could find them a London agent; there was no need to antagonize the man, no need to close doors to opportunity. He, for one, didn't want to end up at that dull teaching job in Arusha. He was speaking as though to everyone, but his eyes were on Ujunwa.

Ujunwa bought a necklace and put it on and liked the look of the white, tooth-shaped pendant against her throat. That evening Isabel smiled when she saw it. "I wish people would see how faux ivory looks real and leave the animals alone," she said. Ujunwa beamed and said that it was in fact real ivory and wondered whether to add that she had killed the elephant herself during a royal hunt. Isabel looked startled, then pained. Ujunwa fingered the plastic. She needed to be relaxed, and she said this to herself over and over, as she started to read from her story. Afterwards, the Ugandan spoke first, saying how strong a story it was, how believable, his confident tone surprising Ujunwa even more than his words. The Tanzanian said she captured Lagos well, the smells and sounds, and it was incredible how similar Third World cities were. The white South African said she hated that term, Third World, but had loved the realistic portrayal of what women were going through in Nigeria. Edward leaned back and said, "It's never quite like that in real life, is it? Women are never victims in that sort of crude way and certainly not in Nigeria. Nigeria has women in high positions. The most powerful cabinet minister today is a woman."

The Kenyan cut in and said he liked the story but didn't believe Chioma would give up the job; she was, after all, a woman with no other choices, and so he thought the ending was implausible.

"The whole thing is implausible," Edward said. "This is agenda writing, it isn't a real story of real people."

Inside Ujunwa, something shrank. Edward was still speaking. Of course one had to admire the writing itself, which was quite *mah*-ve-lous. He was watching her, and it was the victory in his eyes that made her stand up and start to laugh. The participants stared at her. She laughed and laughed and they watched her and then she picked up her papers. "A real story of real people?" she said, with her eyes on Edward's face. "The only thing I didn't add in the story is that after I left my coworker and walked out of the alhaji's house, I got into the Jeep and insisted that the driver take me home because I knew it was the last time I would be riding in it."

There were other things Ujunwa wanted to say, but she did not say them. There were tears crowding up in her eyes but she did not let them out. She was looking forward to calling her mother, and as she walked back to her cabin, she wondered whether this ending, in a story, would be considered plausible.

THE THING AROUND
YOUR NECK

You thought everybody in America had a car and a gun; your uncles and aunts and cousins thought so, too. Right after you won the American visa lottery, they told you: In a month, you will have a big car. Soon, a big house. But don't buy a gun like those Americans.

They trooped into the room in Lagos where you lived with your father and mother and three siblings, leaning against the unpainted walls because there weren't enough chairs to go round, to say goodbye in loud voices and tell you with lowered voices what they wanted you to send them. In comparison to the big car and house (and possibly gun), the things they wanted were minor—handbags and shoes and perfumes and clothes. You said okay, no problem.

Your uncle in America, who had put in the names of all your family members for the American visa lottery, said you could live with him until you got on your feet. He picked you up at the airport and bought you a big hot dog with yellow mustard that nauseated you. Introduction to America, he said with a laugh. He lived in a small white town in Maine, in a thirty-year-old house by a lake. He told you that the company he worked for had offered him a few thousand more than the average salary plus stock options because they were desperately trying to look diverse. They included a photo of him in every brochure, even those that had nothing to do with his unit. He laughed and said the job was good, was worth living in an all-white town even though his wife had to drive an hour to find a hair salon that did black hair. The trick was to understand America, to know that America was give-and-take. You gave up a lot but you gained a lot, too.

He showed you how to apply for a cashier job in the gas station on Main Street and he enrolled you in a community college, where the girls had thick thighs and wore bright-red nail polish, and self-tanner that made them look orange. They asked where you learned to speak English and if you had real houses back in Africa and if you'd seen a car before you came to America. They gawped at your hair. Does it stand up or fall down when you take out the braids? They wanted to know. All of it stands up? How? Why? Do you use a comb? You smiled tightly when they asked those questions. Your uncle told you to expect it; a mixture of ignorance and arrogance, he called it. Then he told you how the neighbors said, a few months after he moved into his house, that the squirrels had started to disappear. They had heard that Africans ate all kinds of wild animals.

You laughed with your uncle and you felt at home in his house; his wife called you *nwanne*, sister, and his two school-age children called you Aunty. They spoke Igbo and ate *garri* for lunch and it was like home. Until your uncle came into the cramped basement where you slept with old boxes and cartons and pulled you forcefully to him, squeezing your buttocks, moaning. He wasn't really your uncle; he was actually a brother of your father's sister's husband, not related by blood. After you pushed him away, he sat on your bed—it was his house, after all—and smiled and said you were no longer a child at twenty-two. If you let him, he would do many things for you. Smart women did it all the time. How did you think those women back home in Lagos with well-paying jobs made it? Even women in New York City?

You locked yourself in the bathroom until he went back upstairs, and the next morning, you left, walking the long windy road, smelling the baby fish in the lake. You saw him drive past—he had always dropped you off at Main Street—and he didn't honk. You wondered what he would tell his wife, why you had left. And you remembered what he said, that America was give-and-take.

You ended up in Connecticut, in another little town, because it was the last stop of the Greyhound bus you got on. You walked into the restaurant with the bright, clean awning and said you would work for two dollars less than the other waitresses. The manager, Juan, had inky-black hair and smiled to show a gold tooth. He said he had never had a Nigerian employee but all immigrants worked hard. He knew, he'd been there. He'd pay you a dollar less, but under the table; he didn't like all the taxes they were making him pay.

You could not afford to go to school, because now you paid rent for the tiny room with the stained carpet. Besides, the small Connecticut town didn't have a community college and credits at the state university cost too much. So you went to the public library, you looked up course syllabi on school Web sites and read some of the books. Sometimes you sat on the lumpy mattress of your twin bed and thought about home—your aunts who hawked dried fish and plantains, cajoling customers to buy and then shouting insults when they didn't; your uncles who drank local gin and crammed their families and lives into single rooms; your friends who had come out to say goodbye before you left, to rejoice because you won the American visa lottery, to confess their envy; your parents who often held hands as they walked to church on Sunday mornings, the neighbors from the next room laughing and teasing them; your father who brought back his boss's old newspapers from work and made your brothers read them; your mother whose salary was barely enough to pay your brothers' school fees at the secondary school where teachers gave an A when someone slipped them a brown envelope.

You had never needed to pay for an A, never slipped a brown envelope to a teacher in secondary school. Still, you chose long brown envelopes to send half your month's earnings to your parents at the address of the parastatal where your mother was a cleaner; you always used the dollar notes that Juan gave you because those were crisp, unlike the tips. Every month. You wrapped the money carefully in white paper but you didn't write a letter. There was nothing to write about.

In later weeks, though, you wanted to write because you had stories to tell. You wanted to write about the surprising openness of people in America, how eagerly they told you about their mother fighting cancer, about their sister-in-law's preemie, the kinds of things that one should hide or should reveal only to the family members who wished them well. You wanted to write about the way people left so much food on their plates and crumpled a few dollar bills down, as though it was an offering, expiation for the wasted food. You wanted to write about the child who started to cry and pull at her blond hair and push the menus off the table and instead of the parents making her shut up, they pleaded with her, a child of perhaps five years old, and then they all got up and left. You wanted to write about the rich people who wore shabby clothes and tattered sneakers, who looked like the night watchmen in front of the large compounds in Lagos. You wanted to write that rich Americans were thin and poor Americans were fat and that many did not have a big house and car; you still were not sure about the guns, though, because they might have them inside their pockets.

It wasn't just to your parents you wanted to write, it was also to your friends, and cousins and aunts and uncles. But you could never afford enough perfumes and clothes and handbags and shoes to go around and still pay your rent on what you earned at the waitressing job, so you wrote nobody.

Nobody knew where you were, because you told no one. Sometimes you felt invisible and tried to walk through your room wall into the hallway, and when you bumped into the wall, it left bruises on your arms. Once, Juan asked if you had a man that hit you because he would take care of him and you laughed a mysterious laugh.

At night, something would wrap itself around your neck, something that very nearly choked you before you fell asleep.

Many people at the restaurant asked when you had come from Jamaica, because they thought that every black person with a foreign accent was Jamaican. Or some who guessed that you were African told you that they loved elephants and wanted to go on a safari.

So when he asked you, in the dimness of the restaurant after you recited the daily specials, what African country you were from, you said Nigeria and expected him to say that he had donated money to fight AIDS in Botswana. But he asked if you were Yoruba or Igbo, because you didn't have a Fulani face. You were surprised—you thought he must be a professor of anthropology at the state university, a little young in his late twenties or so, but who was to say? Igbo, you said. He asked your name and said Akunna was pretty. He did not ask what it meant, fortunately, because you were sick of how people said, " 'Father's Wealth'? You mean, like, your father will actually sell you to a husband?"

He told you he had been to Ghana and Uganda and Tanzania, loved the poetry of Okot p'Bitek and the novels of Amos Tutuola and had read a lot about sub-Saharan African countries, their histories, their complexities. You wanted to feel disdain, to show it as you brought his order, because white people who liked Africa too much and those who liked Africa too little were the same—condescending. But he didn't shake his head in the superior way that Professor Cobbledick back in the Maine community college did during a class discussion on decolonization in Africa. He didn't have that expression of Professor Cobbledick's, that expression of a person who thought himself better than the people he knew about. He came in the next day and sat at the same table and when you asked if the chicken was okay, he asked if you had grown up in Lagos. He came in the third day and began talking before he ordered, about how he had visited Bombay and now wanted to visit Lagos, to see how real people lived, like in the shantytowns, because he never did any of the silly tourist stuff when he was abroad. He talked and talked and you had to tell him it was against restaurant policy. He brushed your hand when you set the glass of water down. The fourth day, when you saw him arrive, you told Juan you didn't want that table anymore. After your shift that night, he was waiting outside, earphones stuck in his ears, asking you to go out with him because your name rhymed with *hakuna matata* and *The Lion King* was the only maudlin movie he'd ever liked. You didn't know what *The Lion King* was. You looked at him in the bright light and noticed that his eyes were the color of extra-virgin olive oil, a greenish gold. Extra-virgin olive oil was the only thing you loved, truly loved, in America.

He was a senior at the state university. He told you how old he was and you asked why he had not graduated yet. This was America, after all, it was not like back home, where universities closed so often that people added three years to their normal course of study and lecturers went on strike after strike and still were not paid. He said he had taken a couple of years off to discover himself and travel, mostly to Africa and Asia. You asked him where he ended up finding himself and he laughed. You did not laugh. You did not know that people could simply choose not to go to school, that people could dictate to life. You were used to accepting what life gave, writing down what life dictated.

You said no the following four days to going out with him, because you were uncomfortable with the way he looked at your face, that intense, consuming way he looked at your face that made you say goodbye to him but also made you reluctant to walk away. And then, the fifth night, you panicked when he was not standing at the door after your shift. You prayed for the first time in a long time and when he came up behind you and said hey, you said yes, you would go out with him, even before he asked. You were scared he would not ask again.

The next day, he took you to dinner at Chang's and your fortune cookie had two strips of paper. Both of them were blank.

You knew you had become comfortable when you told him that you watched *Jeopardy* on the restaurant TV and that you rooted for the following, in this order: women of color, black men, and white women, before, finally, white men—which meant you never rooted for white men. He laughed and told you he was used to not being rooted for, his mother taught women's studies.

And you knew you had become close when you told him that your father was really not a schoolteacher in Lagos, that he was a junior driver for a construction company. And you told him about that day in Lagos traffic in the rickety Peugeot 504 your father drove; it was raining and your seat was wet because of the rust-eaten hole in the roof. The traffic was heavy, the traffic was always heavy in Lagos, and when it rained it was chaos. The roads became muddy ponds and cars got stuck and some of your cousins went out and made some money pushing the cars out. The rain, the swampiness, you thought, made your father step on the brakes too late that day. You heard the bump before you felt it. The car your father rammed into was wide, foreign, and dark green, with golden headlights like the eyes of a leopard. Your father started to cry and beg even before he got out of the car and laid himself flat on the road, causing much blowing of horns. Sorry sir, sorry sir, he chanted. If you sell me and my family, you cannot buy even one tire on your car. Sorry sir.

The Big Man seated at the back did not come out, but his driver did, examining the damage, looking at your father's sprawled form from the corner of his eye as though the pleading was like pornography, a performance he was ashamed to admit he enjoyed. At last he let your father go. Waved him away. The other cars' horns blew and drivers cursed. When your father came back into the car, you refused to look at him because he was just like the pigs that wallowed in the marshes around the market. Your father looked like *nsi*. Shit.

After you told him this, he pursed his lips and held your hand and said he understood how you felt. You shook your hand free, suddenly annoyed, because he thought the world was, or ought to be, full of people like him. You told him there was nothing to understand, it was just the way it was.

He found the African store in the Hartford yellow pages and drove you there. Because of the way he walked around with familiarity, tilting the bottle of palm wine to see how much sediment it had, the Ghanaian store owner asked him if he was African, like the white Kenyans or South Africans, and he said yes, but he'd been in America for a long time. He looked pleased that the store owner had believed him. You cooked that evening with the things you had bought, and after he ate *garri* and *onugbu* soup, he threw up in your sink. You didn't mind, though, because now you would be able to cook *onugbu* soup with meat.

He didn't eat meat because he thought it was wrong the way they killed animals; he said they released fear toxins into the animals and the fear toxins made people paranoid. Back home, the meat pieces you ate, when there was meat, were the size of half your finger. But you did not tell him that. You did not tell him either that the *dawadawa* cubes your mother cooked everything with, because curry and thyme were too expensive, had MSG, *were* MSG. He said MSG caused cancer, it was the reason he liked Chang's; Chang didn't cook with MSG.

Once, at Chang's, he told the waiter he had recently visited Shanghai, that he spoke some Mandarin. The waiter warmed up and told him what soup was best and then asked him, "You have girlfriend in Shanghai now?" And he smiled and said nothing.

You lost your appetite, the region deep in your chest felt clogged. That night, you didn't moan when he was inside you,

you bit your lips and pretended that you didn't come because you knew he would worry. Later you told him why you were upset, that even though you went to Chang's so often together, even though you had kissed just before the menus came, the Chinese man had assumed you could not possibly be his girl-friend, and he had smiled and said nothing. Before he apolo-gized, he gazed at you blankly and you knew that he did not understand.

He bought you presents and when you objected about the cost, he said his grandfather in Boston had been wealthy but hastily added that the old man had given a lot away and so the trust fund he had wasn't huge. His presents mystified you. A fist-size glass ball that you shook to watch a tiny, shapely doll in pink spin around. A shiny rock whose surface took on the color of whatever touched it. An expensive scarf hand-painted in Mex-ico. Finally you told him, your voice stretched in irony, that in your life presents were always useful. The rock, for instance, would work if you could grind things with it. He laughed long and hard but you did not laugh. You realized that in his life, he could buy presents that were just presents and nothing else, nothing useful. When he started to buy you shoes and clothes and books, you asked him not to, you didn't want any presents at all. He bought them anyway and you kept them for your cousins and uncles and aunts, for when you would one day be able to visit home, even though you did not know how you could ever afford a ticket *and* your rent. He said he really wanted to see Nigeria and he could pay for you both to go. You did not want him to pay for you to visit home. You did not want him to go to Nigeria, to add it to the list of countries where he went to gawk at the lives of poor people who could never gawk back at *his* life. You told him this on a sunny day, when he took you to see Long Island Sound, and the two of you argued, your voices raised as you walked along the calm water. He said you were wrong to call him self-righteous. You said he was wrong to call only the poor Indians in Bombay the real Indians. Did it mean he wasn't a real American, since he was not like the poor fat people you and he had seen in Hartford? He hurried ahead of you, his upper body bare and pale, his flip-flops raising bits of sand, but then he came back and held out his hand for yours. You made up and made love and ran your hands through each other's hair, his soft and yellow like the swinging tassels of growing corn, yours dark and bouncy like the filling of a pillow. He had got too much sun and his skin turned the color of a ripe watermelon and you kissed his back before you rubbed lotion on it.

The thing that wrapped itself around your neck, that nearly choked you before you fell asleep, started to loosen, to let go.

You knew by people's reactions that you two were abnormal— the way the nasty ones were too nasty and the nice ones too nice. The old white men and women who muttered and glared at him, the black men who shook their heads at you, the black women whose pitying eyes bemoaned your lack of self-esteem, your self-loathing. Or the black women who smiled swift solidarity smiles; the black men who tried too hard to forgive you, saying a too-obvious hi to him; the white men and women who said "What a good-looking pair" too brightly, too loudly, as though to prove their own open-mindedness to themselves.

But his parents were different; they almost made you think it was all normal. His mother told you that he had never brought a girl to meet them, except for his high school prom date, and he grinned stiffly and held your hand. The tablecloth shielded your clasped hands. He squeezed your hand and you squeezed back and wondered why he was so stiff, why his extra-virgin-olive-oil-colored eyes darkened as he spoke to his parents. His mother was delighted when she asked if you'd read Nawal el Saadawi and you said yes. His father asked how similar Indian food was to Nigerian food and teased you about paying when the check came. You looked at them and felt grateful that they did not examine you like an exotic trophy, an ivory tusk.

Afterwards, he told you about his issues with his parents, how they portioned out love like a birthday cake, how they would give him a bigger slice if only he'd agree to go to law school. You wanted to sympathize. But instead you were angry.

You were angrier when he told you he had refused to go up to Canada with them for a week or two, to their summer cottage in the Quebec countryside. They had even asked him to bring you. He showed you pictures of the cottage and you wondered why it was called a cottage because the buildings that big around your neighborhood back home were banks and churches. You dropped a glass and it shattered on the hardwood of his apartment floor and he asked what was wrong and you said nothing, although you thought a lot was wrong. Later, in the shower, you started to cry. You watched the water dilute your tears and you didn't know why you were crying.

You wrote home finally. A short letter to your parents, slipped in between the crisp dollar bills, and you included your address. You got a reply only days later, by courier. Your mother wrote the letter herself; you knew from the spidery penmanship, from the misspelled words.

Your father was dead; he had slumped over the steering

wheel of his company car. Five months now, she wrote. They had used some of the money you sent to give him a good funeral: They killed a goat for the guests and buried him in a good coffin. You curled up in bed, pressed your knees to your chest, and tried to remember what you had been doing when your father died, what you had been doing for all the months when he was already dead. Perhaps your father died on the day your whole body had been covered in goosebumps, hard as uncooked rice, that you could not explain, Juan teasing you about taking over from the chef so that the heat in the kitchen would warm you up. Perhaps your father died on one of the days you took a drive to Mystic or watched a play in Manchester or had dinner at Chang's.

He held you while you cried, smoothed your hair, and offered to buy your ticket, to go with you to see your family. You said no, you needed to go alone. He asked if you would come back and you reminded him that you had a green card and you would lose it if you did not come back in one year. He said you knew what he meant, would you come back, come back?

You turned away and said nothing, and when he drove you to the airport, you hugged him tight for a long, long moment, and then you let go.

THE AMERICAN EMBASSY

She stood in line outside the American embassy in Lagos, staring straight ahead, barely moving, a blue plastic file of documents tucked under her arm. She was the forty-eighth person in the line of about two hundred that trailed from the closed gates of the American embassy all the way past the smaller, vine-encrusted gates of the Czech embassy. She did not notice the newspaper vendors who blew whistles and pushed *The Guardian, Thenews,* and *The Vanguard* in her face. Or the beggars who walked up and down holding out enamel plates. Or the ice-cream bicycles that honked. She did not fan herself with a magazine or swipe at the tiny fly hovering near her ear. When the man standing behind her tapped her on the back and asked, "Do you have change, *abeg,* two tens for twenty naira?" she stared at him for a while, to focus, to remember where she was, before she shook her head and said, "No."

The air hung heavy with moist heat. It weighed on her head, made it even more difficult to keep her mind blank, which Dr. Balogun had said yesterday was what she would have to do. He had refused to give her any more tranquilizers because she needed to be alert for the visa interview. It was easy enough for him to say that, as though she knew how to go about keeping her mind blank, as though it was in her power, as though she invited those images of her son Ugonna's small, plump body crumpling before her, the splash on his chest so red she wanted to scold him about playing with the palm oil in the kitchen. Not that he could even reach up to the shelf where she kept oils and spices, not that he could unscrew the cap on the plastic bottle of palm oil. He was only four years old.

The man behind her tapped her again. She jerked around and nearly screamed from the sharp pain that ran down her back. Twisted muscle, Dr. Balogun had said, his expression awed that she had sustained nothing more serious after jumping down from the balcony.

"See what that useless soldier is doing there," the man behind her said.

She turned to look across the street, moving her neck slowly. A small crowd had gathered. A soldier was flogging a bespectacled man with a long whip that curled in the air before it landed on the man's face, or his neck, she wasn't sure because the man's hands were raised as if to ward off the whip. She saw the man's glasses slip off and fall. She saw the heel of the soldier's boot squash the black frames, the tinted lenses.

"See how the people are pleading with the soldier," the man behind her said. "Our people have become too used to pleading with soldiers."

She said nothing. He was persistent with his friendliness, unlike the woman in front of her who had said earlier, "I have been talking to you and you just look at me like a moo-moo!" and now ignored her. Perhaps he was wondering why she did not share in the familiarity that had developed among the others in the line. Because they had all woken up early—those who had slept at all—to get to the American embassy before dawn; because they had all struggled for the visa line, dodging the soldiers' swinging whips as they were herded back and forth before the line was finally formed; because they were all afraid that the American embassy might decide not to open its gates today, and they would have to do it all over again the day after tomorrow since the embassy did not open on Wednesdays, they had formed friendships. Buttoned-up men and women exchanged newspapers and denunciations of General Abacha's government, while young people in jeans, bristling with savoir faire, shared tips on ways to answer questions for the American student visa.

"Look at his face, all that bleeding. The whip cut his face," the man behind her said.

She did not look, because she knew the blood would be red, like fresh palm oil. Instead she looked up Eleke Crescent, a winding street of embassies with vast lawns, and at the crowds of people on the sides of the street. A breathing sidewalk. A market that sprung up during the American embassy hours and disappeared when the embassy closed. There was the chair-rental outfit where the stacks of white plastic chairs that cost one hundred naira per hour decreased fast. There were the wooden boards propped on cement blocks, colorfully display-ing sweets and mangoes and oranges. There were the young people who cushioned cigarette-filled trays on their heads with rolls of cloth. There were the blind beggars led by children, singing blessings in English, Yoruba, pidgin, Igbo, Hausa when somebody put money in their plates. And there was, of course, the makeshift photo studio. A tall man standing beside a tripod, holding up a chalk-written sign that read EXCELLENT ONE-HOUR PHOTOS, CORRECT AMERICAN VISA SPECIfiCATIONS. She had had her passport photo taken there, sitting on a rickety stool, and she was not surprised that it came out grainy, with her face much lighter-skinned. But then, she had no choice, she couldn't have taken the photo earlier.

Two days ago she had buried her child in a grave near a vegetable patch in their ancestral hometown of Umunnachi, surrounded by well-wishers she did not remember now. The day before, she had driven her husband in the boot of their Toyota to the home of a friend, who smuggled him out of the country. And the day before that, she hadn't needed to take a passport photo; her life was normal and she had taken Ugonna to school, had bought him a sausage roll at Mr. Biggs, had sung along with Majek Fashek on her car radio. If a fortune-teller had told her that she, in the space of a few days, would no longer recognize her life, she would have laughed. Perhaps even given the fortune-teller ten naira extra for having a wild imagination.

"Sometimes I wonder if the American embassy people look out of their window and enjoy watching the soldiers flogging people," the man behind her was saying. She wished he would shut up. It was his talking that made it harder to keep her mind blank, free of Ugonna. She looked across the street again; the soldier was walking away now, and even from this distance she could see the glower on his face. The glower of a grown man who could flog another grown man if he wanted to, when he wanted to. His swagger was as flamboyant as that of the men who four nights ago broke her back door open and barged in.

Where is your husband? Where is he? They had torn open the wardrobes in the two rooms, even the drawers. She could have told them that her husband was over six feet tall, that he could not possibly hide in a drawer. Three men in black trousers. They had smelled of alcohol and pepper soup, and much later, as she held Ugonna's still body, she knew that she would never eat pepper soup again.

Where has your husband gone? Where? They pressed a gun to her head, and she said, "I don't know, he just left yesterday," standing still even though the warm urine trickled down her legs.

One of them, the one wearing a black hooded shirt who smelled the most like alcohol, had eyes that were startlingly bloodshot, so red they looked painful. He shouted the most, kicked at the TV set. *You know about the story your husband wrote in the newspaper? You know he is a liar? You know people like him should be in jail because they cause trouble, because they don't want Nigeria to move forward?*

He sat down on the sofa, where her husband always sat to watch the nightly news on NTA, and yanked at her so that she landed awkwardly on his lap. His gun poked her waist. *Fine woman, why you marry a troublemaker?* She felt his sickening hardness, smelled the fermentation on his breath.

Leave her alone, the other one said. The one with the bald head that gleamed, as though coated in Vaseline. *Let's go.*

She pried herself free and got up from the sofa, and the man in the hooded shirt, still seated, slapped her behind. It was then that Ugonna started to cry, to run to her. The man in the hooded shirt was laughing, saying how soft her body was, waving his gun. Ugonna was screaming now; he never screamed when he cried, he was not that kind of child. Then the gun went off and the palm oil splash appeared on Ugonna's chest.

"See oranges here," the man in line behind her said, offering her a plastic bag of six peeled oranges. She had not noticed him buy them.

She shook her head. "Thank you."

"Take one. I noticed that you have not eaten anything since morning."

She looked at him properly then, for the first time. A nondescript face with a dark complexion unusually smooth for a man. There was something aspirational about his crisp-ironed shirt and blue tie, about the careful way he spoke English as though he feared he would make a mistake. Perhaps he worked for one of the new-generation banks and was making a much better living than he had ever imagined possible.

"No, thank you," she said. The woman in front turned to glance at her and then went back to talking to some people about a special church service called the American Visa Miracle Ministry.

"You should eat, oh," the man behind her said, although he no longer held out the bag of oranges.

She shook her head again; the pain was still there, somewhere between her eyes. It was as if jumping from the balcony had dislodged some bits and pieces inside her head so that they now clattered painfully. Jumping had not been her only choice, she could have climbed onto the mango tree whose branch reached across the balcony, she could have dashed down the stairs. The men had been arguing, so loudly that they blocked out reality, and she believed for a moment that maybe that popping sound had not been a gun, maybe it was the kind of sneaky thunder that came at the beginning of harmattan, maybe the red splash really was palm oil, and Ugonna had gotten to the bottle somehow and was now playing a fainting game even though it was not a game he had ever played. Then their words pulled her back. *You think she will tell people it was an accident? Is this what Oga asked us to do? A small child! We have to hit the mother. No, that is double trouble. Yes. No, let's go, my friend!*

She had dashed out to the balcony then, climbed over the railing, jumped down without thinking of the two storeys, and crawled into the dustbin by the gate. After she heard the roar of their car driving away, she went back to her flat, smelling of the rotten plantain peels in the dustbin. She held Ugonna's body, placed her cheek to his quiet chest, and realized that she had never felt so ashamed. She had failed him.

"You are anxious about the visa interview, *abi*?" the man behind her asked.

She shrugged, gently, so as not to hurt her back, and forced a vacant smile.

"Just make sure that you look the interviewer straight in the eye as you answer the questions. Even if you make a mistake, don't correct yourself, because they will assume you are lying. I have many friends they have refused, for small-small reasons. Me, I am applying for a visitor's visa. My brother lives in Texas and I want to go for a holiday."

He sounded like the voices that had been around her, people who had helped with her husband's escape and with Ugonna's funeral, who had brought her to the embassy. Don't falter as you answer the questions, the voices had said. Tell them all about Ugonna, what he was like, but don't overdo it, because every day people lie to them to get asylum visas, about dead relatives that were never even born. Make Ugonna real. Cry, but don't cry too much.

"They don't give our people immigrant visas anymore, unless the person is rich by American standards. But I hear people from European countries have no problems getting visas. Are you applying for an immigrant visa or a visitor's?" the man asked.

"Asylum." She did not look at his face; rather, she felt his surprise.

"Asylum? That will be very difficult to prove."

She wondered if he read *The New Nigeria,* if he knew about her husband. He probably did. Everyone supportive of the pro-democracy press knew about her husband, especially because he was the first journalist to publicly call the coup plot a sham, to write a story accusing General Abacha of inventing a coup so that he could kill and jail his opponents. Soldiers had come to the newspaper office and carted away large numbers of that edition in a black truck; still, photocopies got out and circulated throughout Lagos—a neighbor had seen a copy pasted on the wall of a bridge next to posters announcing church crusades and new films. The soldiers had detained her husband for two weeks and broken the skin on his forehead, leaving a scar the shape of an L. Friends had gingerly touched the scar when they gathered at their flat to celebrate his release, bringing bottles of whiskey. She remembered somebody saying to him, *Nigeria will be well because of you,* and she remembered her husband's expression, that look of the excited messiah, as he talked about the soldier who had given him a cigarette after beating him, all the while stammering in the way he did when he was in high spirits. She had found that stammer endearing years ago; she no longer did.

"Many people apply for asylum visa and don't get it," the man behind her said. Loudly. Perhaps he had been talking all the while.

"Do you read *The New Nigeria?*" she asked. She did not turn to face the man, instead she watched a couple ahead in the line buy packets of biscuits; the packets crackled as they opened them.

"Yes. Do you want it? The vendors may still have some copies."

"No. I was just asking."

"Very good paper. Those two editors, they are the kind of people Nigeria needs. They risk their lives to tell us the truth. Truly brave men. If only we had more people with that kind of courage."

It was not courage, it was simply an exaggerated selfishness. A month ago, when her husband forgot about his cousin's wedding even though they had agreed to be wedding sponsors, telling her he could not cancel his trip to Kaduna because his interview with the arrested journalist there was too important, she had looked at him, the distant, driven man she had married, and said, "You are not the only one who hates the government." She went to the wedding alone and he went to Kaduna, and when he came back, they said little to each other; much of their conversation had become about Ugonna, anyway. You will not believe what this boy did today, she would say when he came home from work, and then go on to recount in detail how Ugonna had told her that there was pepper in his Quaker Oats and so he would no longer eat it, or how he had helped her draw the curtains.

"So you think what those editors do is bravery?" She turned to face the man behind her.

"Yes, of course. Not all of us can do it. That is the real problem with us in this country, we don't have enough brave people." He gave her a long look, righteous and suspicious, as though he was wondering if she was a government apologist, one of those people who criticized the pro-democracy movements, who maintained that only a military government would work in Nigeria. In different circumstances, she might have told him of her own journalism, starting from university in Zaria, when she had organized a rally to protest General Buhari's government's decision to cut student subsidies. She might have told him how she wrote for the *Evening News* here in Lagos, how she did the story on the attempted murder of the publisher of *The Guardian,* how she had resigned when she finally got pregnant, because she and her husband had tried for four years and she had a womb full of fibroids.

She turned away from the man and watched the beggars make their rounds along the visa line. Rangy men in grimy long tunics who fingered prayer beads and quoted the Koran; women with jaundiced eyes who had sickly babies tied to their backs with threadbare cloth; a blind couple led by their daughter, blue medals of the Blessed Virgin Mary hanging around their necks below tattered collars. A newspaper vendor walked over, blowing his whistle. She could not see *The New Nigeria* among the papers balanced on his arm. Perhaps it had sold out. Her husband's latest story, "The Abacha Years So Far: 1993 to 1997," had not worried her at first, because he had written nothing new, only compiled killings and failed contracts and missing money. It was not as if Nigerians did not already know these things. She had not expected much trouble, or much attention, but only a day after the paper came out, BBC radio carried the story on the news and interviewed an exiled Nigerian professor of politics who said her husband deserved a Human Rights Award. *He fights repression with the pen, he gives a voice to the voiceless, he makes the world know.*

Her husband had tried to hide his nervousness from her. Then, after someone called him anonymously—he got anonymous calls all the time, he was that kind of journalist, the kind who cultivated friendships along the way—to say that the head of state was personally furious, he no longer hid his fear; he let her see his shaking hands. Soldiers were on their way to arrest him, the caller said. The word was, it would be his last arrest, he would never come back. He climbed into the boot of the car minutes after the call, so that if the soldiers asked, the gateman could honestly claim not to know when her husband had left. She took Ugonna down to a neighbor's flat and then quickly sprinkled water in the boot, even though her husband told her to hurry, because she felt somehow that a wet boot would be cooler, that he would breathe better. She drove him to his coeditor's house. The next day, he called her from Benin Republic; the coeditor had contacts who had sneaked him over the border. His visa to America, the one he got when he went for a training course in Atlanta, was still valid, and he would apply for asylum when he arrived in New York. She told him not to worry, she and Ugonna would be fine, she would apply for a visa at the end of the school term and they would join him in America. That night, Ugonna was restless and she let him stay up and play with his toy car while she read a book. When she saw the three men burst in through the kitchen door, she hated herself for not insisting that Ugonna go to bed. If only—

"Ah, this sun is not gentle at all. These American Embassy people should at least build a shade for us. They can use some of the money they collect for visa fee," the man behind her said.

Somebody behind him said the Americans were collecting the money for their own use. Another person said it was intentional to keep applicants waiting in the sun. Yet another laughed. She motioned to the blind begging couple and fumbled in her bag for a twenty-naira note. When she put it in the bowl, they chanted, "God bless you, you will have money, you will have good husband, you will have good job," in Pidgin English and then in Igbo and Yoruba. She watched them walk away. They had not told her, "You will have many good children." She had heard them tell that to the woman in front of her.

The embassy gates swung open and a man in a brown uniform shouted, "First fifty on the line, come in and fill out the forms. All the rest, come back another day. The embassy can attend to only fifty today."

"We are lucky, *abi?*" the man behind her said.

She watched the visa interviewer behind the glass screen, the way her limp auburn hair grazed the folded neck, the way green eyes peered at her papers above silver frames as though the glasses were unnecessary.

"Can you go through your story again, ma'am? You haven't given me any details," the visa interviewer said with an encouraging smile. This, she knew, was her opportunity to talk about Ugonna.

She looked at the next window for a moment, at a man in a dark suit who was leaning close to the screen, reverently, as though praying to the visa interviewer behind. And she realized that she would die gladly at the hands of the man in the black hooded shirt or the one with the shiny bald head before she said a word about Ugonna to this interviewer, or to anybody at the American embassy. Before she hawked Ugonna for a visa to safety.

Her son had been killed, that was all she would say. Killed. Nothing about how his laughter started somehow above his head, high and tinkly. How he called sweets and biscuits "breadie-breadie." How he grasped her neck tight when she held him. How her husband said that he would be an artist because he didn't try to build with his LEGO blocks but instead he arranged them, side by side, alternating colors. They did not deserve to know.

"Ma'am? You say it was the government?" the visa interviewer asked.

"Government" was such a big label, it was freeing, it gave people room to maneuver and excuse and re-blame. Three men. Three men like her husband or her brother or the man behind her on the visa line. Three men.

"Yes. They were government agents," she said.

"Can you prove it? Do you have any evidence to show that?"

"Yes. But I buried it yesterday. My son's body."

"Ma'am, I am sorry about your son," the visa interviewer said. "But I need some evidence that you know it was the government. There is fighting going on between ethnic groups, there are private assassinations. I need some evidence of the government's involvement and I need some evidence that you will be in danger if you stay on in Nigeria."

She looked at the faded pink lips, moving to show tiny teeth. Faded pink lips in a freckled, insulated face. She had the urge to ask the visa interviewer if the stories in *The New Nigeria* were worth the life of a child. But she didn't. She doubted that the visa interviewer knew about pro-democracy newspapers or about the long, tired lines outside the embassy gates in cordoned-off areas with no shade where the furious sun caused friendships and headaches and despair.

"Ma'am? The United States offers a new life to victims of political persecution but there needs to be proof . . ."

A new life. It was Ugonna who had given her a new life, surprised her by how quickly she took to the new identity he gave her, the new person he made her. "I'm Ugonna's mother," she would say at his nursery school, to teachers, to parents of other children. At his funeral in Umunnachi, because her friends and family had been wearing dresses in the same Ankara print, somebody had asked, "Which one is the mother?" and she had looked up, alert for a moment, and said, "I'm Ugonna's mother." She wanted to go back to their ancestral hometown and plant ixora flowers, the kind whose needle-thin stalks she had sucked as a child. One plant would do, his plot was so small. When it bloomed, and the flowers welcomed bees, she wanted to pluck and suck at them while squatting in the dirt. And afterwards, she wanted to arrange the sucked flowers side by side, like Ugonna had done with his LEGO blocks. That, she realized, was the new life she wanted.

At the next window, the American visa interviewer was speaking too loudly into his microphone, "I'm not going to accept your lies, sir!"

The Nigerian visa applicant in the dark suit began to shout and to gesture, waving his see-through plastic file that bulged with documents. "This is wrong! How can you treat people like this? I will take this to Washington!" until a security guard came and led him away.

"Ma'am? Ma'am?"

Was she imagining it, or was the sympathy draining from the visa interviewer's face? She saw the swift way the woman pushed her reddish-gold hair back even though it did not disturb her, it stayed quiet on her neck, framing a pale face. Her future rested on that face. The face of a person who did not understand her, who probably did not cook with palm oil, or know that palm oil when fresh was a bright, bright red and when not fresh, congealed to a lumpy orange.

She turned slowly and headed for the exit.

"Ma'am?" she heard the interviewer's voice behind her.

She didn't turn. She walked out of the American embassy, past the beggars who still made their rounds with enamel bowls held outstretched, and got into her car.

THE SHIVERING

On the day a plane crashed in Nigeria, the same day the Nigerian first lady died, somebody knocked loudly on Ukamaka's door in Princeton. The knock surprised her because nobody ever came to her door unannounced—this after all was America, where people called before they visited—except for the FedEx man, who never knocked that loudly; and it made her jumpy because since morning she had been on the Internet reading Nigerian news, refreshing pages too often, calling her parents and her friends in Nigeria, making cup after cup of Earl Grey that she allowed to get cold. She had minimized early pictures from the crash site. Each time she looked at them, she brightened her laptop screen, peering at what the news articles called "wreckage," a blackened hulk with whitish bits scattered all about it like torn paper, an indifferent lump of char that had once been a plane filled with people—people who buckled their seat belts and prayed, people who unfolded newspapers, people who waited for the flight attendant to roll down a cart and ask, "Sandwich or cake?" One of those people might have been her ex-boyfriend Udenna.

The knock sounded again, louder. She looked through the

peephole: a pudgy, dark-skinned man who looked vaguely familiar though she could not remember where she had seen him before. Perhaps it was at the library or on the shuttle to the Princeton campus. She opened the door. He half-smiled and spoke without meeting her eye. "I am Nigerian. I live on the third floor. I came so that we can pray about what is happening in our country."

She was surprised that he knew she, too, was Nigerian, that he knew which apartment was hers, that he had come to knock on her door; she still could not place where she had seen him before.

"Can I come in?" he asked.

She let him in. She let into her apartment a stranger wearing a slack Princeton sweatshirt who had come to pray about what was happening in Nigeria, and when he reached out to take her hands in his, she hesitated slightly before extending hers. They prayed. He prayed in that particularly Nigerian Pente-costal way that made her uneasy: he covered things with the blood of Jesus, he bound up demons and cast them in the sea, he battled evil spirits. She wanted to interrupt and tell him how unnecessary it was, this bloodying and binding, this turning faith into a pugilistic exercise; to tell him that life was a struggle with ourselves more than with a spear-wielding Satan; that belief was a choice for our conscience always to be sharpened. But she did not say these words, because they would sound sanctimonious coming from her; she would not be able to give them that redeeming matter-of-fact dryness as Father Patrick so easily did.

"Jehova God, all the machinations of the Evil One shall not succeed, all the weapons fashioned against us shall not prosper, in the name of Jesus! Father Lord, we cover all the planes in Nigeria with the precious blood of Jesus; Father Lord, we cover the air with the precious blood of Jesus and we destroy all the agents of darkness. . . ." His voice was getting louder, his head bobbing. She needed to urinate. She felt awkward with their hands clasped together, his fingers warm and firm, and it was her discomfort that made her say, the first time he paused after a breathless passage, "Amen!" thinking that it was over, but it was not and so she hastily closed her eyes again as he continued. He prayed and prayed, pumping her hands whenever he said "Father Lord!" or "in Jesus' name!"

Then she felt herself start to shiver, an involuntary quivering of her whole body. Was it God? Once, years ago when she was a teenager who meticulously said the rosary every morning, words she did not understand had burst out of her mouth as she knelt by the scratchy wooden frame of her bed. It had lasted mere seconds, that outpouring of incomprehensible words in the middle of a Hail Mary, but she had truly, at the end of the rosary, felt terrified and sure that the white-cool feeling that enveloped her was God. Udenna was the only person she had ever told about it, and he said she had created the experience herself. But how could I have? she had asked. How could I have created something I did not even want? Yet, in the end, she agreed with him, as she always agreed with him about almost anything, and said that she had indeed imagined it all.

Now, the shivering stopped as quickly as it had started and the Nigerian man ended the prayer. "In the mighty and ever-lasting name of Jesus!"

"Amen!" she said.

She slipped her hands from his, mumbled "Excuse me," and hurried into the bathroom. When she came out, he was still standing by the door in the kitchen. There was something about his demeanor, the way he stood with his arms folded, that made her think of the word "humble."

"My name is Chinedu," he said.

"I'm Ukamaka," she said.

They shook hands, and this amused her because they had only just clasped each other's hands in prayer.

"This plane crash is terrible," he said. "Very terrible."

"Yes." She did not tell him that Udenna might have been in the crash. She wished he would leave, now that they had prayed, but he moved across into the living room and sat down on the couch and began to talk about how he first heard of the plane crash as if she had asked him to stay, as if she needed to know the details of his morning ritual, that he listened to BBC News online because there was never anything of substance in American news. He told her he did not realize at first that there were two separate incidents—the first lady had died in Spain shortly after a tummy-tuck surgery in preparation for her sixtieth birthday party, while the plane had crashed in Lagos minutes after it left for Abuja.

"Yes," she said, and sat down in front of her laptop. "At first I thought she died in the crash, too."

He was rocking himself slightly, his arms still folded. "The coincidence is too much. God is telling us something. Only God can save our country."

Us. Our country. Those words united them in a common loss, and for a moment she felt close to him. She refreshed an Internet page. There was still no news of any survivors.

"God has to take control of Nigeria," he went on. "They said that a civilian government would be better than the military ones, but look at what Obasanjo is doing. He has seriously destroyed our country."

She nodded, wondering what would be the most polite way to ask him to leave, and yet reluctant to do so, because his presence gave her hope about Udenna being alive, in a way that she could not explain.

"Have you seen pictures of family members of the victims? One woman tore her clothes off and ran around in her slip. She said her daughter was on that flight, and that her daughter was going to Abuja to buy fabric for her. *Chai!*" Chinedu let out the long sucking sound that showed sadness. "The only friend I know who might have been on that flight just sent me an e-mail to say he is fine, thank God. None of my family members would have been on it, so at least I don't have to worry about them. They don't have ten thousand naira to throw away on a plane ticket!" He laughed, a sudden inappropriate sound. She refreshed an Internet page. Still no news.

"I know somebody who was on the flight," she said. "Who might have been on the flight."

"Jehova God!"

"My boyfriend Udenna. My ex-boyfriend, actually. He was doing an MBA at Wharton and went to Nigeria last week for his cousin's wedding." It was after she spoke that she realized she had used the past tense.

"You have not heard anything for sure?" Chinedu asked.

"No. He doesn't have a cell phone in Nigeria and I can't get through to his sister's phone. Maybe she was with him. The wedding is supposed to be tomorrow in Abuja."

They sat in silence; she noticed that Chinedu's hands had tightened into fists, that he was no longer rocking himself.

"When was the last time you spoke to him?" he asked.

"Last week. He called before he left for Nigeria."

"God is faithful. God is faithful!" Chinedu raised his voice. "God is faithful. Do you hear me?"

A little alarmed, Ukamaka said, "Yes."

The phone rang. Ukamaka stared at it, the black cordless phone she had placed next to her laptop, afraid to pick it up. Chinedu got up and made to reach for it and she said "No!" and took it and walked to the window. "Hello? Hello?" She wanted whomever it was to tell her right away, not to start with any preambles. It was her mother.

"*Nne,* Udenna is fine. Chikaodili just called me to say they missed the flight. He is fine. They were supposed to be on that flight but they missed it, thank God."

Ukamaka put the phone down on the window ledge and began to weep. First, Chinedu gripped her shoulders, then he took her in his arms. She quieted herself long enough to tell him Udenna was fine and then went back into his embrace, surprised by the familiar comfort of it, certain that he instinctively understood her crying from the relief of what had not happened and from the melancholy of what could have happened and from the anger of what remained unresolved since Udenna told her, in an ice-cream shop on Nassau Street, that the relationship was over.

"I knew my God would deliver! I have been praying in my heart for God to keep him safe," Chinedu said, rubbing her back.

Later, after she had asked Chinedu to stay for lunch and as she heated up some stew in the microwave, she asked him, "If you say God is responsible for keeping Udenna safe, then it means God is responsible for the people who died, because God could have kept them safe, too. Does it mean God prefers some people to others?"

"God's ways are not our ways." Chinedu took off his sneakers and placed them by the bookshelf.

"It doesn't make sense."

"God always makes sense but not always a human kind of sense," Chinedu said, looking at the photos on her bookshelf. It was the kind of question she asked Father Patrick, although Father Patrick would agree that God did not always make sense, with that shrug of his, as he did the first time she met him, on that late summer day Udenna told her it was over. She and Udenna had been inside Thomas Sweet, drinking strawberry and banana smoothies, their Sunday ritual after grocery shopping, and Udenna had slurped his noisily before he told her that their relationship had been over for a long time, that they were together only out of habit, and she looked at him and waited for a laugh, although it was not his style to joke like that. "Staid" was the word he had used. There was nobody else, but the relationship had become staid. Staid, and yet she had been arranging her life around his for three years. Staid, and yet she had begun to bother her uncle, a senator, about finding her a job in Abuja after she graduated because Udenna wanted to move back when he finished graduate school and start building up what he called "political capital" for his run for Anambra State governor. Staid, and yet she cooked her stews with hot peppers now, the way he liked. Staid, and yet they had spoken often about the children they would have, a boy and a girl whose conception she had taken for granted, the girl to be named Ulari and the boy Udoka, all their first names to be U-names. She left Thomas Sweet and began to walk aimlessly all the way up Nassau Street and then back down again until she passed the gray stone church and she wandered in and told the man wearing a white collar and just about to climb into his Subaru that life did not make sense. He told her his name was Father Patrick and that life did not make sense but we all had to have faith nonetheless. Have faith. "Have faith" was like saying be tall and shapely. She wanted to be tall and shapely but of course she was not; she was short and her behind was flat and that stubborn soft bit of her lower belly bulged, even when she wore her Spanx body-shaper, with its tightly restraining fabric. When she said this, Father Patrick laughed.

" 'Have faith' is not really like saying be tall and shapely. It's more like saying be okay with the bulge and with having to wear Spanx," he said. And she had laughed, too, surprised that this plump white man with silver hair knew what Spanx was.

Ukamaka dished out some stew beside the already warmed rice on Chinedu's plate. "If God prefers some people to others, it doesn't make sense that it would be Udenna who would be spared. Udenna could not have been the nicest or kindest person who was booked on that flight," she said.

"You can't use human reasoning for God." Chinedu held up the fork she had placed on his plate. "Please give me a spoon."

She handed him one. Udenna would have been amused by Chinedu, would have said how very bush it was to eat rice with a spoon the way Chinedu did, gripping it with all his fingers— Udenna with his ability to glance at people and know, from their posture and their shoes, what kind of childhood they had had.

"That's Udenna, right?" Chinedu gestured toward the photo in the wicker frame, Udenna's arm draped around her shoulders, both their faces open and smiling; it had been taken by a stranger at a restaurant in Philadelphia, a stranger who had said, "You are such a lovely couple, are you married?" and Udenna had replied, "Not yet," in that flirty crooked-smile way he had with female strangers.

"Yes, that is the great Udenna." Ukamaka made a face and settled down at the tiny dining table with her plate. "I keep forgetting to remove that picture." It was a lie. She had glanced at it often in the past month, sometimes reluctantly, always frightened of the finality of taking it down. She sensed that Chinedu knew it was a lie.

"Did you meet in Nigeria?" he asked.

"No, we met at my sister's graduation party three years ago in New Haven. A friend of hers brought him. He was working on Wall Street and I was already in grad school here but we knew many of the same people from around Philadelphia. He went to UPenn for undergrad and I went to Bryn Mawr. It's funny that we had so much in common but somehow we had never met until then. Both of us came to the U.S. to go to university at about the same time. It turned out we even took the SATs at the same center in Lagos and on the same day!"

"He looks tall," Chinedu said, still standing by the bookcase, his plate balanced in his hand.

"He's six feet four." She heard the pride in her own voice. "That's not his best picture. He looks a lot like Thomas Sankara. I had a crush on that man when I was a teenager. You know, the president of Burkina Faso, the popular president, the one they killed—"

"Of course I know Thomas Sankara." Chinedu looked closely at the photograph for a moment, as though to search for traces of Sankara's famed handsomeness. Then he said, "I saw both of you once outside in the parking lot and I knew you were from Nigeria. I wanted to come and introduce myself but I was in a rush to catch the shuttle."

Ukamaka was pleased to hear this; his having seen them together made the relationship tangible. The past three years of sleeping with Udenna and aligning her plans to Udenna's and cooking with peppers were not, after all, in her imagination. She restrained herself from asking what exactly Chinedu remembered: Had he seen Udenna's hand placed on her lower back? Had he seen Udenna saying something suggestive to her, their faces close together?

"When did you see us?" she asked.

"About two months ago. You were walking toward your car."

"How did you know we were Nigerian?"

"I can always tell." He sat down opposite her. "But this morning I looked at the names on the mailboxes to find out which apartment was yours."

"I remember now that I once saw you on the shuttle. I knew you were African but I thought you might be from Ghana. You looked too gentle to be Nigerian."

Chinedu laughed. "Who says I am gentle?" He mockingly puffed out his chest, his mouth full of rice. Udenna would have pointed out Chinedu's forehead and said that one did not need to hear Chinedu's accent to know that he was the sort of person who had gone to a community secondary school in his village and learned English by reading a dictionary in candlelight, because one could tell right away from his lumpy and vein-scarred forehead. It was what Udenna had said about the Nigerian student at Wharton whose friendship he consistently snubbed, whose e-mails he never replied to. The student, with his giveaway forehead and bush ways, simply did not make the cut. Make the cut. Udenna often used that expression and she at first thought it puerile but had begun, in the last year, to use it herself.

"Is the stew too peppery?" she asked, noticing how slowly Chinedu was eating.

"It's fine. I'm used to eating pepper. I grew up in Lagos."

"I never liked hot food until I met Udenna. I'm not even sure I like it now."

"But you still cook with it."

She did not like his saying that and she did not like that his face was closed, his expression unreadable, as he glanced at her and then back at his plate. She said, "Well, I guess I'm used to it now."

"Can you check for the latest news?"

She pressed a key on her laptop, refreshed a Web page. *All Killed in Nigeria Plane Crash.* The government had confirmed that all one hundred and seventeen people aboard the airplane were dead.

"No survivors," she said.

"Father, take control," Chinedu said, exhaling loudly. He came and sat beside her to read from her laptop, their bodies close, the smell of her peppery stew on his breath. There were more photographs from the crash site. Ukamaka stared at one of shirtless men carrying a piece of metal that looked like the twisted frame of a bed; she could not imagine what part of the plane it could possibly have been.

"There is too much iniquity in our country," Chinedu said, getting up. "Too much corruption. Too many things that we have to pray about."

"Are you saying the crash was a punishment from God?"

"A punishment and a wake-up call." Chinedu was eating the last of his rice. She found it distracting when he scraped the spoon against his teeth.

"I used to go to church every day when I was a teen-ager, morning Mass at six. I did it by myself, my family was a Sunday-Sunday family," she said. "Then one day I just stopped going."

"Everybody has a crisis of faith. It's normal."

"It wasn't a crisis of faith. Church suddenly became like Father Christmas, something that you never question when you are a child but when you become an adult you realize that the man in that Father Christmas costume is actually your neighbor from down the street."

Chinedu shrugged, as though he did not have much patience for this decadence, this ambivalence of hers. "Is the rice finished?"

"There's more." She took his plate to warm up some more rice and stew. When she handed it to him, she said, "I don't know what I would have done if Udenna had died. I don't even know what I would have felt."

"You just have to be grateful to God."

She walked to the window and adjusted the blinds. It was newly autumn. Outside, she could see the trees that lined Lawrence Drive, their foliage a mix of green and copper.

"Udenna never said 'I love you' to me because he thought it was a cliché. Once I told him I was sorry he felt bad about something and he started shouting and said I should not use an expression like 'I'm sorry you feel that way' because it was unoriginal. He used to make me feel that nothing I said was witty enough or sarcastic enough or smart enough. He was always struggling to be different, even when it didn't matter. It was as if he was performing his life instead of living his life."

Chinedu said nothing. He took full mouthfuls; sometimes he used a finger as a wedge to nudge more rice onto his spoon.

"He knew I loved being here, but he was always telling me how Princeton was a boring school, and that it was out of touch. If he thought I was too happy about something that did not have to do with him, he always found a way to put it down. How can you love somebody and yet want to manage the amount of happiness that person is allowed?"

Chinedu nodded; he both understood her and sided with her, she could tell. In the following days, days now cool enough for her knee-length leather boots, days in which she took the shuttle to campus, researched her dissertation at the library, met with her advisor, taught her undergraduate composition class, or met with students asking for permission to hand in assignments late, she would return to her apartment in the late evening and wait for Chinedu to visit so she could offer him rice or pizza or spaghetti. So she could talk about Udenna. She told Chinedu things she could not or did not want to tell Father Patrick. She liked that Chinedu said little, looking as if he was not only listening to her but also thinking about what she was saying. Once she thought idly of starting an affair with him, of indulging in the classic rebound, but there was a refreshingly asexual quality to him, something about him that made her feel that she did not have to pat some powder under her eyes to hide her dark circles.

Her apartment building was full of other foreigners. She and Udenna used to joke that it was the uncertainty of the foreigners' new surroundings that had congealed into the indifference they showed to one another. They did not say hello in the hallways or elevators, nor did they meet one another's eyes during the five-minute ride on the campus shuttle, these intellectual stars from Kenya and China and Russia, these graduate students and fellows who would go on to lead and heal and reinvent the world. And so it surprised her that as she and Chinedu walked to the parking lot, he would wave to somebody, say hi to another. He told her about the Japanese post-doc fellow who sometimes gave him a ride to the mall, the German doctoral student whose two-year-old daughter called him Chindle.

"Do you know them from your program?" she asked, and then added, "What program are you in?"

He had once said something about chemistry, and she

assumed he was doing a doctorate in chemistry. It had to be why she never saw him on campus; the science labs were so far off and so alien.

"No. I met them when I came here."

"How long have you lived here?"

"Not long. Since spring."

"When I first came to Princeton, I wasn't sure I wanted to live in a house only for grad students and fellows, but I kind of like it now. The first time Udenna visited me, he said this square building was so ugly and charmless. Were you in graduate housing before?"

"No." Chinedu paused and looked away. "I knew I had to make the effort to make friends in this building. How else will I get to the grocery store and to church? Thank God you have a car," he said.

She liked that he had said "Thank God you have a car," because it was a statement about friendship, about doing things together in the long term, about having somebody who would listen to her talk about Udenna.

On Sundays, she drove Chinedu to his Pentecostal church in Lawrenceville before going to the Catholic church on Nassau Street, and when she picked him up after service, they went grocery shopping at McCaffrey's. She noticed how few groceries he bought and how carefully he scoured the sale flyers that Udenna had always ignored.

When she stopped at Wild Oats, where she and Udenna had bought organic vegetables, Chinedu shook his head in wonder because he did not understand why anybody would pay more money for the same vegetables just because they had been grown without chemicals. He was examining the grains displayed in large plastic dispensers while she selected broccoli and put it in a bag.

"Chemical-free this. Chemical-free that. People are wasting money for nothing. Aren't the medicines they take to stay alive chemicals, too?"

"You know it's not the same thing, Chinedu."

"I don't see the difference."

Ukamaka laughed. "It doesn't really matter to me either way, but Udenna always wanted us to buy organic fruits and vegetables. I think he had read somewhere that it was what somebody like him was supposed to buy."

Chinedu looked at her with that unreadable closed expression again. Was he judging her? Trying to make up his mind about something he thought of her?

She said, as she opened the trunk to put in the grocery bag, "I'm starving. Should we get a sandwich somewhere?"

"I'm not hungry."

"It's my treat. Or do you prefer Chinese?"

"I'm fasting," he said quietly.

"Oh." As a teenager, she, too, had fasted, drinking only water from morning until evening for a whole week, asking God to help her get the best result in the Senior Secondary School exam. She got the third-best result.

"No wonder you didn't eat any rice yesterday," she said. "Will you sit with me while I eat then?"

"Sure."

"Do you fast often, or is this a special prayer you are doing? Or is it too personal for me to ask?"

"It is too personal for you to ask," Chinedu said with a mocking solemnity.

She took down the car windows as she backed out of Wild Oats, stopping to let two jacketless women walk past, their jeans tight, their blond hair blown sideways by the wind. It was a strangely warm day for late autumn.

"Fall sometimes reminds me of harmattan," Chinedu said.

"I know," Ukamaka said. "I love harmattan. I think it's because of Christmas. I love the dryness and dust of Christmas. Udenna and I went back together for Christmas last year and he spent New Year's Day with my family in Nimo and my uncle kept questioning him: 'Young man, when will you bring your family to come and knock on our door? What are you studying in school?' " Ukamaka mimicked a gruff voice and Chinedu laughed.

"Have you gone home to visit since you left?" Ukamaka asked, and as soon as she did, she wished she had not. Of course he would not have been able to afford a ticket home to visit.

"No." His tone was flat.

"I was planning to move back after graduate school and work with an NGO in Lagos, but Udenna wanted to go into politics, so I started planning to live in Abuja instead. Will you move back when you finish here? I can imagine the loads of money you'll make at one of those oil companies in the Niger Delta, with your chemistry doctorate." She knew she was speaking too fast, babbling, really, trying to make up for the discomfort she had felt earlier.

"I don't know." Chinedu shrugged. "Can I change the radio station?"

"Of course." She sensed his mood shift in the way he kept his eyes focused on the window after he changed the radio from NPR to an FM station with loud music.

"I think I'll get your favorite, sushi, instead of a sandwich," she said, her tone teasing. She had once asked if he liked sushi and he had said, "God forbid. I am an African man. I eat only cooked food." She added, "You really should try sushi sometime. How can you live in Princeton and not eat sashimi?"

He barely smiled. She drove slowly to the sandwich place,

over-nodding to the music from the radio to show that she was enjoying it as he seemed to be.

"I'll just pick up the sandwich," she said, and he said he would wait in the car. The garlic flavors from the foil-wrapped chicken sandwich filled the car when she got back in.

"Your phone rang," Chinedu said.

She picked up her cell phone, lodged by the shift, and looked at it. Rachel, a friend from her department, perhaps calling to find out if she wanted to go to the talk on morality and the novel at East Pyne the next day.

"I can't believe Udenna hasn't called me," she said, and started the car. He had sent an e-mail to thank her for her concern while he was in Nigeria. He had removed her from his Instant Messenger buddy list so that she could no longer know when he was online. And he had not called.

"Maybe it's best for him not to call," Chinedu said. "So you can move on."

"It's not that simple," she said, slightly annoyed, because she wanted Udenna to call, because the photo was still up on her bookcase, because Chinedu sounded as if he alone knew what was best for her. She waited until they were back at their apartment building and Chinedu had taken his bags up to his apartment and come back down before she said, "You know, it really isn't as simple as you think it is. You don't know what it is to love an asshole."

"I do."

She looked at him, wearing the same clothes he had worn the afternoon he first knocked on her door: a pair of jeans and an old sweatshirt with a saggy neckline, PRINCETON printed on the front in orange.

"You've never said anything about it," she said.

"You've never asked."

She placed her sandwich on a plate and sat down at the tiny dining table. "I didn't know there was anything to ask. I thought you would just tell me."

Chinedu said nothing.

"So tell me. Tell me about this love. Was it here or back home?"

"Back home. I was with him for almost two years."

The moment was quiet. She picked up a napkin and realized that she had known intuitively, perhaps from the very beginning, but she said, because she thought he expected her to show surprise, "Oh, you're gay."

"Somebody once told me that I am the straightest gay person she knew, and I hated myself for liking that." He was smiling; he looked relieved.

"So tell me about this love."

The man's name was Abidemi. Something about the way Chinedu said his name, Abidemi, made her think of gently pressing on a sore muscle, the kind of self-inflicted ache that is satisfying.

He spoke slowly, revising details that she thought made no difference—was it on a Wednesday or Thursday that Abidemi had taken him to a private gay club where they shook hands with a former head of state?—and she thought that this was a story he had not told often in its entirety, perhaps had never told. He talked as she finished her sandwich and sat beside him on the couch and she felt oddly nostalgic about the details of Abidemi: he drank Guinness stout, he sent his driver to buy roast plantains from the roadside hawkers, he went to House on the Rock Pentecostal church, he liked the Lebanese kibbe at Double Four restaurant, he played polo.

Abidemi was a banker, a Big Man's son who had gone to university in England, the kind of guy who wore leather belts with elaborate designer logos as buckles. He had been wearing one of those when he came into the Lagos office of the mobile phone company where Chinedu worked in customer service. He had been almost rude, asking if there wasn't somebody senior he could talk to, but Chinedu did not miss the look they exchanged, the heady thrill he had not felt since his first relationship with a sports prefect in secondary school. Abidemi gave him his card and said, curtly, "Call me." It was the way Abidemi would run the relationship for the next two years, wanting to know where Chinedu went and what he did, buying him a car without consulting him, so that he was left in the awkward position of explaining to his family and friends how he had suddenly bought a Honda, asking him to come on trips to Calabar and Kaduna with only a day's notice, sending vicious text messages when Chinedu missed his calls. Still, Chinedu had liked the possessiveness, the vitality of a relationship that consumed them both. Until Abidemi said he was getting married. Her name was Kemi and his parents and hers had known one another a long time. The inevitability of marriage had always been understood between them, unspoken but understood, and perhaps nothing would have changed if Chinedu had not met Kemi, at Abidemi's parents' wedding anniversary party. He had not wanted to go to the party—he stayed away from Abidemi's family events—but Abidemi had insisted, saying he would survive the long evening only if Chinedu was there. Abidemi spoke in a voice lined with what seemed troublingly like laughter when he introduced Chinedu to Kemi as "my very good friend."

"Chinedu drinks much more than I do," Abidemi had said to Kemi, with her long weave-on and strapless yellow dress. She sat next to Abidemi, reaching out from time to time to brush something off his shirt, to refill his glass, to place a hand on his knee, and all the while her whole body was braced and attuned to his, as though ready to spring up and do whatever it took to please him. "You said I will grow a beer belly, *abi*?" Abidemi said, his hand on her thigh. "This man will grow one before me, I'm telling you."

Chinedu had smiled tightly, a tension headache starting, his rage at Abidemi exploding. As Chinedu told Ukamaka this, how the anger of that evening had "scattered his head," she noticed how tense he had become.

"You wished you hadn't met his wife," Ukamaka said.

"No. I wished he had been conflicted."

"He must have been."

"He wasn't. I watched him that day, the way he was with both of us there, drinking stout and making jokes about me to her and about her to me, and I knew he would go to bed and sleep well at night. If we continued, he would come to me and then go home to her and sleep well every night. I wanted him not to sleep well sometimes."

"And you ended it?"

"He was angry. He did not understand why I would not do what he wanted."

"How can a person claim to love you and yet want you to do things that suit only them? Udenna was like that."

Chinedu squeezed the pillow on his lap. "Ukamaka, not everything is about Udenna."

"I'm just saying that Abidemi sounds a little bit like Udenna. I guess I just don't understand that kind of love."

"Maybe it wasn't love," Chinedu said, standing up abruptly from the couch. "Udenna did this to you and Udenna did that to you, but why did you let him? Why did you let him? Have you ever considered that it wasn't love?"

It was so savagely cold, his tone, that for a moment Ukamaka felt frightened, then she felt angry and told him to get out of her apartment.

She had begun, before that day, to notice strange things about Chinedu. He never asked her up to his apartment, and once, after he told her which apartment was his, she looked at the mailbox and was surprised that it did not have his last name on it; the building superintendent was very strict about all the names of renters being on the mailbox. He did not ever seem to go to campus; the only time she asked him why, he had said something deliberately vague, which told her he did not want to talk about it, and she let it go because she suspected that he had academic problems, perhaps was grappling with a dissertation that was going nowhere. And so, a week after she asked him to get out of her apartment, a week of not speaking to him, she went up and knocked on his door, and when he opened it and looked at her warily, she asked, "Are you working on a dissertation?"

"I'm busy," he said, shortly, and closed the door in her face.

She stood there for a while before going back to her apartment. She would never speak to him again, she told herself; he was a crude and rude person from the bush. But Sunday came and she had become used to driving him to his church in Lawrenceville before going to hers on Nassau Street. She hoped he would knock on her door and yet knew that he would not. She felt a sudden fear that he would ask somebody else on his floor to drop him off at church, and because she felt her fear becoming a panic, she went up and knocked on his door. It took him a while to open. He looked drawn and tired; his face was unwashed and ashy.

"I'm sorry," she said. "That question about whether you are working on a dissertation was just my stupid way of saying I'm sorry."

"Next time if you want to say you're sorry just say you're sorry."

"Do you want me to drop you off at church?"

"No." He gestured for her to come in. The apartment was sparsely furnished with a couch, a table, and a TV; books were piled one on top of the other along the walls.

"Look, Ukamaka, I have to tell you what's happening. Sit down."

She sat down. A cartoon show was on TV, a Bible open face-down on the table, a cup of what looked like coffee next to it.

"I am out of status. My visa expired three years ago. This apartment belongs to a friend. He is in Peru for a semester and he said I should come and stay while I try to sort myself out."

"You're not here at Princeton?"

"I never said I was." He turned away and closed the Bible. "I'm going to get a deportation notice from Immigration any-time soon. Nobody at home knows my real situation. I haven't been able to send them much since I lost my construction job. My boss was a nice man and was paying me under the table but he said he did not want trouble now that they are talking about raiding workplaces."

"Have you tried finding a lawyer?" she asked.

"A lawyer for what? I don't have a case." He was biting his lower lip, and she had not seen him look so unattractive before, with his flaking facial skin and his shadowed eyes. She would not ask for more details because she knew he was unwilling to tell her more.

"You look terrible. You haven't eaten much since I last

saw you," she said, thinking of all the weeks that she had spent talking about Udenna while Chinedu worried about being deported.

"I'm fasting."

"Are you sure you don't want me to drop you off at church?"

"It's too late anyway."

"Come with me to my church then."

"You know I don't like the Catholic Church, all that unnecessary kneeling and standing and worshiping idols."

"Just this once. I'll go to yours with you next week."

Finally he got up and washed his face and changed into a clean sweater. They walked to the car in silence. She had never thought to tell him about her shivering as he prayed on that first day, but because she longed now for a significant gesture that would show him that he was not alone; that she understood what it must be like to feel so uncertain of a future, to lack control about what would happen to him tomorrow—because she did not, in fact, know what else to say—she told him about the shivering.

"It was strange," she said. "Maybe it was just my suppressed anxiety about Udenna."

"It was a sign from God," Chinedu said firmly.

"What was the point of my shivering as a sign from God?"

"You have to stop thinking that God is a person. God is God."

"Your faith, it's almost like fighting." She looked at him. "Why can't God reveal himself in an unambiguous way and clear things up once and for all? What's the point of God being a puzzle?"

"Because it is the nature of God. If you understand the basic idea of God's nature being different from human nature, then it will make sense," Chinedu said, and opened the door to climb out of the car. What a luxury to have a faith like his, Ukamaka thought, so uncritical, so forceful, so impatient. And yet there was something about it that was exceedingly fragile; it was as if Chinedu could conceive of faith only in extremes, as if an acknowledgment of a middle ground would mean the risk of losing everything.

"I see what you mean," she said, although she did not see at all, although it was answers like his that, years back, had made her decide to stop going to church, and kept her away until the Sunday Udenna used "staid" in an ice-cream shop on Nassau Street.

Outside the gray stone church, Father Patrick was greeting people, his hair a gleaming silver in the late morning light.

"I'm bringing a new person into the dungeon of Catholicism, Father P.," Ukamaka said.

"There's always room in the dungeon," Father Patrick said, warmly shaking Chinedu's hand, saying welcome.

The church was dim, full of echoes and mysteries and the faint scent of candles. They sat side by side in the middle row, next to a woman holding a baby.

"Did you like him?" Ukamaka whispered.

"The priest? He seemed okay."

"I mean like like."

"Oh, Jehova God! Of course not."

She had made him smile. "You are not going to be deported, Chinedu. We will find a way. We will." She squeezed his hand and knew he was amused by her stressing of the "we."

He leaned close. "You know, I had a crush on Thomas Sankara, too."

"No!" Laughter was bubbling up in her chest.

"I didn't even know that there was a country called Burkina Faso in West Africa until my teacher in secondary school talked about him and brought in a picture. I will never forget how crazy in love I fell with a newspaper photograph."

"Don't tell me Abidemi sort of looks like him."

"Actually he does."

At first they stifled their laughter and then they let it out, joyously leaning against each other, while next to them, the woman holding the baby watched.

The choir had begun to sing. It was one of those Sundays when the priest blessed the congregation with holy water at the beginning of Mass, and Father Patrick was walking up and down, flicking water on the people with something that looked like a big saltshaker. Ukamaka watched him and thought how much more subdued Catholic Masses were in America; how in Nigeria it would have been a vibrant green branch from a mango tree that the priest would dip in a bucket of holy water held by a hurrying, sweating Mass-server; how he would have stridden up and down, splashing and swirling, holy water raining down; how the people would have been drenched; and how, smiling and making the sign of the cross, they would have felt blessed.

THE ARRANGERS
OF MARRIAGE

My new husband carried the suitcase out of the taxi and led the way into the brownstone, up a flight of brooding stairs, down an airless hallway with frayed carpeting, and stopped at a door. The number 2B, unevenly fashioned from yellowish metal, was plastered on it.

"We're here," he said. He had used the word "house" when he told me about our home. I had imagined a smooth driveway snaking between cucumber-colored lawns, a door leading into a hallway, walls with sedate paintings. A house like those of the white newlyweds in the American films that NTA showed on Saturday nights.

He turned on the light in the living room, where a beige couch sat alone in the middle, slanted, as though dropped there by accident. The room was hot; old, musty smells hung heavy in the air.

"I'll show you around," he said.

The smaller bedroom had a bare mattress lodged in one corner. The bigger bedroom had a bed and dresser, and a phone on the carpeted floor. Still, both rooms lacked a sense of space, as though the walls had become uncomfortable with each other, with so little between them.

"Now that you're here, we'll get more furniture. I didn't need that much when I was alone," he said.

"Okay," I said. I felt light-headed. The ten-hour flight from Lagos to New York and the interminable wait while the American customs officer raked through my suitcase had left me woozy, stuffed my head full of cotton wool. The officer had examined my foodstuffs as if they were spiders, her gloved fingers poking at the waterproof bags of ground *egusi* and dried *onugbu* leaves and *uziza* seeds, until she seized my *uziza* seeds. She feared I would grow them on American soil. It didn't matter that the seeds had been sun-dried for weeks and were as hard as a bicycle helmet.

"Ike agwum," I said, placing my handbag down on the bedroom floor.

"Yes, I'm exhausted, too," he said. "We should get to bed."

In the bed with sheets that felt soft, I curled up tight like Uncle Ike's fist when he is angry and hoped that no wifely duties would be required of me. I relaxed moments later when I heard my new husband's measured snoring. It started like a deep rumble in his throat, then ended on a high pitch, a sound like a lewd whistle. They did not warn you about things like this when they arranged your marriage. No mention of offensive snoring, no mention of houses that turned out to be furniture-challenged flats.

My husband woke me up by settling his heavy body on top of mine. His chest flattened my breasts.

"Good morning," I said, opening sleep-crusted eyes. He grunted, a sound that might have been a response to my greeting or part of the ritual he was performing. He raised himself to pull my nightdress up above my waist.

"Wait—" I said, so that I could take the nightdress off, so it would not seem so hasty. But he had crushed his mouth down on mine. Another thing the arrangers of marriage failed to mention—mouths that told the story of sleep, that felt clammy like old chewing gum, that smelled like the rubbish dumps at Ogbete Market. His breathing rasped as he moved, as if his nostrils were too narrow for the air that had to be let out. When he finally stopped thrusting, he rested his entire weight on me, even the weight of his legs. I did not move until he climbed off me to go into the bathroom. I pulled my nightdress down, straightened it over my hips.

"Good morning, baby," he said, coming back into the room. He handed me the phone. "We have to call your uncle and aunt to tell them we arrived safely. Just for a few minutes; it costs almost a dollar a minute to Nigeria. Dial 011 and then 234 before the number."

"*Ezi okwu?* All that?"

"Yes. International dialing code first and then Nigeria's country code."

"Oh," I said. I punched in the fourteen numbers. The stickiness between my legs itched.

The phone line crackled with static, reaching out across the Atlantic. I knew Uncle Ike and Aunty Ada would sound warm, they would ask what I had eaten, what the weather in America was like. But none of my responses would register; they would ask just to ask. Uncle Ike would probably smile into the phone, the same kind of smile that had loosened his face when he told me that the perfect husband had been found for me. The same smile I had last seen on him months before when the Super Eagles won the soccer gold medal at the Atlanta Olympics.

"A doctor in America," he had said, beaming. "What could be better? Ofodile's mother was looking for a wife for him, she was very concerned that he would marry an American. He hadn't been home in eleven years. I gave her a photo of you. I did not hear from her for a while and I thought they had found someone. But . . ." Uncle Ike let his voice trail away, let his beaming get wider.

"Yes, Uncle."

"He will be home in early June," Aunty Ada had said. "You will have plenty of time to get to know each other before the wedding."

"Yes, Aunty." "Plenty of time" was two weeks.

"What have we not done for you? We raise you as our own and then we find you an *ezigbo di*! A doctor in America! It is like we won a lottery for you!" Aunty Ada said. She had a few strands of hair growing on her chin and she tugged at one of them as she spoke.

I had thanked them both for everything—finding me a husband, taking me into their home, buying me a new pair of shoes every two years. It was the only way to avoid being called ungrateful. I did not remind them that I wanted to take the JAMB exam again and try for the university, that while going to secondary school I had sold more bread in Aunty Ada's bakery than all the other bakeries in Enugu sold, that the furniture and floors in the house shone because of me.

"Did you get through?" my new husband asked.

"It's engaged," I said. I looked away so that he would not see the relief on my face.

"Busy. Americans say busy, not engaged," he said. "We'll try later. Let's have breakfast."

For breakfast, he defrosted pancakes from a bright-yellow bag. I watched what buttons he pressed on the white microwave, carefully memorizing them.

"Boil some water for tea," he said

"Is there some dried milk?" I asked, taking the kettle to the sink. Rust clung to the sides of the sink like peeling brown paint.

"Americans don't drink their tea with milk and sugar."

"*Ezi okwu?* Don't you drink yours with milk and sugar?"

"No, I got used to the way things are done here a long time ago. You will too, baby."

I sat before my limp pancakes—they were so much thinner than the chewy slabs I made at home—and bland tea that I feared would not get past my throat. The doorbell rang and he got up. He walked with his hands swinging to his back; I had not really noticed that before, I had not had time to notice.

"I heard you come in last night." The voice at the door was American, the words flowed fast, ran into each other. *Supri-supri,* Aunty Ify called it, fast-fast. "When you come back to visit, you will be speaking *supri-supri* like Americans," she had said.

"Hi, Shirley. Thanks so much for keeping my mail," he said.

"Not a problem at all. How did your wedding go? Is your wife here?"

"Yes, come and say hello."

A woman with hair the color of metal came into the living room. Her body was wrapped in a pink robe knotted at the waist. Judging from the lines that ran across her face, she could have been anything from six decades to eight decades old; I had not seen enough white people to correctly gauge their ages.

"I'm Shirley from 3A. Nice to meet you," she said, shaking my hand. She had the nasal voice of someone battling a cold.

"You are welcome," I said.

Shirley paused, as though surprised. "Well, I'll let you get back to breakfast," she said. "I'll come down and visit with you when you've settled in."

Shirley shuffled out. My new husband shut the door. One of the dining table legs was shorter than the rest, and so the table rocked, like a seesaw, when he leaned on it and said, "You should say 'Hi' to people here, not 'You're welcome.' "

"She's not my age mate."

"It doesn't work that way here. Everybody says hi."

"*O di mma.* Okay."

"I'm not called Ofodile here, by the way. I go by Dave," he said, looking down at the pile of envelopes Shirley had given him. Many of them had lines of writing on the envelope itself, above the address, as though the sender had remembered to add something only after the envelope was sealed.

"Dave?" I knew he didn't have an English name. The invitation cards to our wedding had read *Ofodile Emeka Udenwa and Chinaza Agatha Okafor.*

"The last name I use here is different, too. Americans have a hard time with Udenwa, so I changed it."

"What is it?" I was still trying to get used to Udenwa, a name I had known only a few weeks.

"It's Bell."

"Bell!" I had heard about a Waturuocha that changed to Waturu in America, a Chikelugo that took the more American-friendly Chikel, but from Udenwa to Bell? "That's not even close to Udenwa," I said.

He got up. "You don't understand how it works in this country. If you want to get anywhere you have to be as mainstream as possible. If not, you will be left by the roadside. You have to use your English name here."

"I never have, my English name is just something on my birth certificate. I've been Chinaza Okafor my whole life."

"You'll get used to it, baby," he said, reaching out to caress my cheek. "You'll see."

When he filled out a Social Security number application for me the next day, the name he entered in bold letters was AGATHA BELL.

Our neighborhood was called Flatbush, my new husband told me, as we walked, hot and sweaty, down a noisy street that smelled of fish left out too long before refrigeration. He wanted to show me how to do the grocery shopping and how to use the bus.

"Look around, don't lower your eyes like that. Look around. You get used to things faster that way," he said.

I turned my head from side to side so he would see that I was following his advice. Dark restaurant windows promised the BEST CARIBBEAN AND AMERICAN FOOD in lopsided print, a car wash across the street advertised $3.50 washes on a chalkboard nestled among Coke cans and bits of paper. The sidewalk was chipped away at the edges, like something nibbled at by mice.

Inside the air-conditioned bus, he showed me where to pour in the coins, how to press the tape on the wall to signal my stop.

"This is not like Nigeria, where you shout out to the conductor," he said, sneering, as though he was the one who had invented the superior American system.

Inside Key Food, we walked from aisle to aisle slowly. I was wary when he put a beef pack in the cart. I wished I could touch the meat, to examine its redness, as I often did at Ogbete Market, where the butcher held up fresh-cut slabs buzzing with flies.

"Can we buy those biscuits?" I asked. The blue packets of Burton's Rich Tea were familiar; I did not want to eat biscuits but I wanted something familiar in the cart.

"Cookies. Americans call them cookies," he said.

I reached out for the biscuits (cookies).

"Get the store brand. They're cheaper, but still the same thing," he said, pointing at a white packet.

"Okay," I said. I no longer wanted the biscuits, but I put the store brand in the cart and stared at the blue packet on the shelf, at the familiar grain-embossed Burton's logo, until we left the aisle.

"When I become an Attending, we will stop buying store brands, but for now we have to; these things may seem cheap but they add up," he said.

"When you become a Consultant?"

"Yes, but it's called an Attending here, an Attending Physician."

The arrangers of marriage only told you that doctors made a lot of money in America. They did not add that before doctors started to make a lot of money, they had to do an internship and a residency program, which my new husband had not completed. My new husband had told me this during our short in-flight conversation, right after we took off from Lagos, before he fell asleep.

"Interns are paid twenty-eight thousand a year but work about eighty hours a week. It's like three dollars an hour," he had said. "Can you believe it? Three dollars an hour!"

I did not know if three dollars an hour was very good or very bad—I was leaning toward very good—until he added that even high school students working part-time made much more.

"Also when I become an Attending, we will not live in a neighborhood like this," my new husband said. He stopped to let a woman with her child tucked into her shopping cart pass by. "See how they have bars so you can't take the shopping carts out? In the good neighborhoods, they don't have them. You can take your shopping cart all the way to your car."

"Oh," I said. What did it matter that you could or could not take the carts out? The point was, there *were* carts.

"Look at the people who shop here; they are the ones who immigrate and continue to act as if they are back in their countries." He gestured, dismissively, toward a woman and her two children, who were speaking Spanish. "They will never move forward unless they adapt to America. They will always be doomed to supermarkets like this."

I murmured something to show I was listening. I thought about the open market in Enugu, the traders who sweet-talked you into stopping at their zinc-covered sheds, who were prepared to bargain all day to add one single kobo to the price. They wrapped what you bought in plastic bags when they had them, and when they did not have them, they laughed and offered you worn newspapers.

My new husband took me to the mall; he wanted to show me as much as he could before he started work on Monday. His car rattled as he drove, as though there were many parts that had come loose—a sound similar to shaking a tin full of nails. It stalled at a traffic light and he turned the key a few times before it started.

"I'll buy a new car after my residency," he said.

Inside the mall, the floors gleamed, smooth as ice cubes, and the high-as-the-sky ceiling blinked with tiny ethereal lights. I felt as though I were in a different physical world, on another planet. The people who pushed against us, even the black ones, wore the mark of foreignness, otherness, on their faces.

"We'll get pizza first," he said. "It's one thing you have to like in America."

We walked up to the pizza stand, to the man wearing a nose ring and a tall white hat.

"Two pepperoni and sausage. Is your combo deal better?" my new husband asked. He sounded different when he spoke to Americans: his *r* was overpronounced and his *t* was underpronounced. And he smiled, the eager smile of a person who wanted to be liked.

We ate the pizza sitting at a small round table in what he called a "food court." A sea of people sitting around circular tables, hunched over paper plates of greasy food. Uncle Ike would be horrified at the thought of eating here; he was a titled man and did not even eat at weddings unless he was served in a private room. There was something humiliatingly public, something lacking in dignity, about this place, this open space of too many tables and too much food.

"Do you like the pizza?" my new husband asked. His paper plate was empty.

"The tomatoes are not cooked well."

"We overcook food back home and that is why we lose all the nutrients. Americans cook things right. See how healthy they all look?"

I nodded, looking around. At the next table, a black woman with a body as wide as a pillow held sideways smiled at me. I smiled back and took another pizza bite, tightening my stomach so it would not eject anything.

We went into Macy's afterwards. My new husband led the way toward a sliding staircase; its movement was rubbery-smooth and I knew I would fall down the moment I stepped on it.

"*Biko,* don't they have a lift instead?" I asked. At least I had once ridden in the creaky one in the local government office, the one that quivered for a full minute before the doors rolled open.

"Speak English. There are people behind you," he whispered, pulling me away, toward a glass counter full of twinkling jewelry. "It's an elevator, not a lift. Americans say elevator."

"Okay."

He led me to the lift (elevator) and we went up to a section lined with rows of weighty-looking coats. He bought me a coat the color of a gloomy day's sky, puffy with what felt like foam inside its lining. The coat looked big enough for two of me to snugly fit into it.

"Winter is coming," he said. "It is like being inside a freezer, so you need a warm coat."

"Thank you."

"Always best to shop when there is a sale. Sometimes you get the same thing for less than half the price. It's one of the wonders of America."

"*Ezi okwu?*" I said, then hastily added, "Really?"

"Let's take a walk around the mall. There are some other wonders of America here."

We walked, looking at stores that sold clothes and tools and plates and books and phones, until the bottoms of my feet ached.

Before we left, he led the way to McDonald's. The restaurant was nestled near the rear of the mall; a yellow and red M the size of a car stood at its entrance. My husband did not look at the menu board that hovered overhead as he ordered two large Number 2 meals.

"We could go home so I can cook," I said. "Don't let your husband eat out too much," Aunty Ada had said, "or it will push him into the arms of a woman who cooks. Always guard your husband like a guinea fowl's egg."

"I like to eat this once in a while," he said. He held the hamburger with both hands and chewed with a concentration that furrowed his eyebrows, tightened his jaw, and made him look even more unfamiliar.

I made coconut rice on Monday, to make up for the eating out. I wanted to make pepper soup, too, the kind Aunty Ada said softened a man's heart. But I needed the *uziza* that the customs officer had seized; pepper soup was just not pepper soup without it. I bought a coconut in the Jamaican store down the street and spent an hour cutting it into tiny bits because there was no grater, and then soaked it in hot water to extract the juice. I had just finished cooking when he came home. He wore what looked like a uniform, a girlish-looking blue top tucked into a pair of blue trousers that was tied at the waist.

"Nno," I said. "Did you work well?"

"You have to speak English at home, too, baby. So you can get used to it." He brushed his lips against my cheek just as the doorbell rang. It was Shirley, her body wrapped in the same pink robe. She twirled the belt at her waist.

"That smell," she said, in her phlegm-filled voice. "It's everywhere, all over the building. What are you cooking?"

"Coconut rice," I said.

"A recipe from your country?"

"Yes."

"It smells really good. The problem with us here is we have no culture, no culture at all." She turned to my new husband, as if she wanted him to agree with her, but he simply smiled. "Would you come take a look at my air conditioner, Dave?" She asked. "It's acting up again and it's so hot today."

"Sure," my new husband said.

Before they left, Shirley waved at me and said, "Smells *really* good," and I wanted to invite her to have some rice. My new husband came back half an hour later and ate the fragrant meal I placed before him, even smacking his lips like Uncle Ike sometimes did to show Aunty Ada how pleased he was with her cooking. But the next day, he came back with a *Good Housekeeping All-American Cookbook,* thick as a Bible.

"I don't want us to be known as the people who fill the building with smells of foreign food," he said.

I took the cookbook, ran my hand over the cover, over the picture of something that looked like a flower but was probably food.

"I know you'll soon master how to cook American food," he said, gently pulling me close. That night, I thought of the cookbook as he lay heavily on top of me, grunting and rasping. Another thing the arrangers of marriage did not tell you—the struggle to brown beef in oil and dredge skinless chicken in flour. I had always cooked beef in its own juices. Chicken I had always poached with its skin intact. In the following days, I was pleased that my husband left for work at six in the morning and did not come back until eight in the evening so that I had time to throw away pieces of half-cooked, clammy chicken and start again.

.   .   .

The first time I saw Nia, who lived in 2D, I thought she was the kind of woman Aunty Ada would disapprove of. Aunty Ada would call her an *ashawo,* because of the see-through top she wore so that her bra, a mismatched shade, glared through. Or Aunty Ada would base her prostitute judgment on Nia's lipstick, a shimmery orange, and the eye shadow—similar to the shade of the lipstick—that clung to her heavy lids.

"Hi," she said when I went down to get the mail. "You're Dave's new wife. I've been meaning to come over and meet you. I'm Nia."

"Thanks. I'm Chinaza . . . Agatha."

Nia was watching me carefully. "What was the first thing you said?"

"My Nigerian name."

"It's an Igbo name, isn't it?" She pronounced it "E-boo."

"Yes."

"What does it mean?"

"God answers prayers."

"It's really pretty. You know, Nia is a Swahili name. I changed my name when I was eighteen. I spent three years in Tanzania. It was fucking amazing."

"Oh," I said and shook my head; she, a black American, had chosen an African name, while my husband made me change mine to an English one.

"You must be bored to death in that apartment; I know Dave gets back pretty late," she said. "Come have a Coke with me."

I hesitated, but Nia was already walking to the stairs. I followed her. Her living room had a spare elegance: a red sofa, a slender potted plant, a huge wooden mask hanging on the wall. She gave me a Diet Coke served in a tall glass with ice, asked how I was adjusting to life in America, offered to show me around Brooklyn.

"It would have to be a Monday, though," she said. "I don't work Mondays."

"What do you do?"

"I own a hair salon."

"Your hair is beautiful," I said, and she touched it and said, "Oh, this," as if she did not think anything of it. It was not just her hair, held up on top of her head in a natural Afro puff, that I found beautiful, though, it was her skin the color of roasted groundnuts, her mysterious and heavy-lidded eyes, her curved hips. She played her music a little too loud, so we had to raise our voices as we spoke.

"You know, my sister's a manager at Macy's," she said. "They're hiring entry-level salespeople in the women's department, so if you're interested I can put in a word for you and you're pretty much hired. She owes me one."

Something leaped inside me at the thought, the sudden and new thought, of earning what would be mine. Mine.

"I don't have my work permit yet," I said.

"But Dave has filed for you?"

"Yes."

"It shouldn't take long; at least you should have it before winter. I have a friend from Haiti who just got hers. So let me know as soon as you do."

"Thank you." I wanted to hug Nia. "Thank you."

That evening I told my new husband about Nia. His eyes were sunken in with fatigue, after so many hours at work, and he said, "Nia?" as though he did not know who I meant, before he added, "She's okay, but be careful because she can be a bad influence."

Nia began stopping by to see me after work, drinking from a can of diet soda she brought with her and watching me cook. I turned the air conditioner off and opened the window to let in the hot air, so that she could smoke. She talked about the women at her hair salon and the men she went out with. She sprinkled her everyday conversation with words like the noun "clitoris" and the verb "fuck." I liked to listen to her. I liked the way she smiled to show a tooth that was chipped neatly, a perfect triangle missing at the edge. She always left before my new husband came home.

Winter sneaked up on me. One morning I stepped out of the apartment building and gasped. It was as though God was shredding tufts of white tissue and flinging them down. I stood staring at my first snow, at the swirling flakes, for a long, long time before turning to go back into the apartment. I scrubbed the kitchen floor again, cut out more coupons from the Key Food catalog that came in the mail, and then sat by the window, watching God's shredding become frenzied. Winter had come and I was still unemployed. When my husband came home in the evening, I placed his french fries and fried chicken before him and said, "I thought I would have my work permit by now."

He ate a few pieces of oily-fried potatoes before responding. We spoke only English now; he did not know that I spoke Igbo to myself while I cooked, that I had taught Nia how to say "I'm hungry" and "See you tomorrow" in Igbo.

"The American woman I married to get a green card is making trouble," he said, and slowly tore a piece of chicken in two. The area under his eyes was puffy. "Our divorce was almost final, but not completely, before I married you in Nigeria. Just a minor thing, but she found out about it and now she's threatening to report me to Immigration. She wants more money."

"You were married before?" I laced my fingers together because they had started to shake.

"Would you pass that, please?" he asked, pointing to the lemonade I had made earlier.

"The jug?"

"Pitcher. Americans say pitcher, not jug."

I pushed the jug (pitcher) across. The pounding in my head was loud, filling my ears with a fierce liquid. "You were married before?"

"It was just on paper. A lot of our people do that here. It's business, you pay the woman and both of you do paperwork together but sometimes it goes wrong and either she refuses to divorce you or she decides to blackmail you."

I pulled the pile of coupons toward me and started to rip them in two, one after the other. "Ofodile, you should have let me know this before now."

He shrugged. "I was going to tell you."

"I deserved to know before we got married." I sank down on the chair opposite him, slowly, as if the chair would crack if I didn't.

"It wouldn't have made a difference. Your uncle and aunt had decided. Were you going to say no to people who have taken care of you since your parents died?"

I stared at him in silence, shredding the coupons into smaller and smaller bits; broken-up pictures of detergents and meat packs and paper towels fell to the floor.

"Besides, with the way things are messed up back home, what would you have done?" he asked. "Aren't people with master's degrees roaming the streets, jobless?" His voice was flat.

"Why did you marry me?" I asked.

"I wanted a Nigerian wife and my mother said you were a good girl, quiet. She said you might even be a virgin." He smiled. He looked even more tired when he smiled. "I probably should tell her how wrong she was." •

I threw more coupons on the floor, clasped my hands together, and dug my nails into my skin.

"I was happy when I saw your picture," he said, smacking his lips. "You were light-skinned. I had to think about my children's looks. Light-skinned blacks fare better in America."

I watched him eat the rest of the batter-covered chicken, and I noticed that he did not finish chewing before he took a sip of water.

That evening, while he showered, I put only the clothes he hadn't bought me, two embroidered boubous and one caftan, all Aunty Ada's cast-offs, in the plastic suitcase I had brought from Nigeria and went to Nia's apartment.

Nia made me tea, with milk and sugar, and sat with me at her round dining table that had three tall stools around it.

"If you want to call your family back home, you can call them from here. Stay as long as you want; I'll get on a payment plan with Bell Atlantic."

"There's nobody to talk to at home," I said, staring at the pear-shaped face of the sculpture on the wooden shelf. It's hollow eyes stared back at me.

"How about your aunt?" Nia asked.

I shook my head. You left your husband? Aunty Ada would shriek. Are you mad? Does one throw away a guinea fowl's egg? Do you know how many women would offer both eyes for a doctor in America? For any husband at all? And Uncle Ike would bellow about my ingratitude, my stupidity, his fist and face tightening, before dropping the phone.

"He should have told you about the marriage, but it wasn't a real marriage, Chinaza," Nia said. "I read a book that says we don't fall in love, we climb up to love. Maybe if you gave it time—"

"It's not about that."

"I know," Nia said with a sigh. "Just trying to be fucking positive here. Was there someone back home?"

"There was once, but he was too young and he had no money."

"Sounds really fucked-up."

I stirred my tea although it did not need stirring. "I wonder why my husband had to find a wife in Nigeria."

"You never say his name, you never say Dave. Is that a cultural thing?"

"No." I looked down at the table mat made with waterproof fabric. I wanted to say that it was because I didn't know his name, because I didn't know him.

"Did you ever meet the woman he married? Or did you know any of his girlfriends?" I asked.

Nia looked away. The kind of dramatic turning of head that speaks, that intends to speak, volumes. The silence stretched out between us.

"Nia?" I asked finally.

"I fucked him, almost two years ago, when he first moved in. I fucked him and after a week it was over. We never dated. I never saw him date anybody."

"Oh," I said, and sipped my tea with milk and sugar.

"I had to be honest with you, get everything out."

"Yes," I said. I stood up to look out of the window. The

world outside seemed mummified into a sheet of dead whiteness. The sidewalks had piles of snow the height of a six-year-old child.

"You can wait until you get your papers and then leave," Nia said. "You can apply for benefits while you get your shit together, and then you'll get a job and find a place and support yourself and start afresh. This is the U.S. of fucking A., for God's sake."

Nia came and stood beside me, by the window. She was right, I could not leave yet. I went back across the hall the next evening. I rang the doorbell and he opened the door, stood aside, and let me pass.

TOMORROW
IS TOO FAR

It was the last summer you spent in Nigeria, the summer
before your parents' divorce, before your mother swore you
would never again set foot in Nigeria to see your father's
family, especially Grandmama. You remember the heat of that
summer clearly, even now, eighteen years later—the way
Grandmama's yard felt moistly warm, a yard with so many trees
that the telephone wire was tangled in leaves and different
branches touched one another and sometimes mangoes
appeared on cashew trees and guavas on mango trees. The thick
mat of decaying leaves was soggy under your bare feet. In the
afternoons, yellow-bellied bees buzzed around your head and
your brother Nonso's and cousin Dozie's heads, and in the
evenings Grandmama let only your brother Nonso climb the
trees to shake a loaded branch, although you were a better
climber than he was. Fruits would rain down, avocados and
cashews and guavas, and you and your cousin Dozie would fill
old buckets with them.

It was the summer Grandmama taught Nonso how to pluck
the coconuts. The coconut trees were hard to climb, so limb-
free and tall, and Grandmama gave Nonso a long stick and

showed him how to nudge the padded pods down. She didn't show you, because she said girls never plucked coconuts. Grandmama cracked the coconuts against a stone, carefully, so the watery milk stayed in the lower piece, a jagged cup. Everybody got a sip of the wind-cooled milk, even the children from down the street who came to play, and Grandmama presided over the sipping ritual to make sure Nonso went first.

It was the summer you asked Grandmama why Nonso sipped first even though Dozie was thirteen, a year older than Nonso, and Grandmama said Nonso was her son's only son, the one who would carry on the Nnabuisi name, while Dozie was only a *nwadiana,* her daughter's son. It was the summer you found the molt of a snake on the lawn, unbroken and sheer like see-through stockings, and Grandmama told you the snake was called the *echi eteka,* "Tomorrow Is Too Far." One bite, she said, and it's over in ten minutes.

It was *not* the summer you fell in love with your cousin Dozie because that happened a few summers before, when he was ten and you were seven and you both wiggled into the tiny space behind Grandmama's garage and he tried to fit what you both called his "banana" into what you both called your "tomato" but neither of you was sure which was the right hole. It was, however, the summer you got lice, and you and your cousin Dozie dug through your thick hair to find the tiny black insects and squash them against your fingernails and laugh at the tart sound of their blood-filled bellies bursting; the summer that your hate for your brother Nonso grew so much you felt it squeezing your nostrils and your love for your cousin Dozie ballooned and wrapped around your skin.

It was the summer you watched a mango tree crack into two

near-perfect halves during a thunderstorm, when the lightning cut fiery lines through the sky.

It was the summer Nonso died.

Grandmama did not call it summer. Nobody did in Nigeria. It was August, nestled between the rainy season and the harmattan season. It could pour all day, silver rain splashing onto the verandah where you and Nonso and Dozie slapped away mosquitoes and ate roast corn; or the sun would be blinding and you would float in the water tank Grandmama had sawed in half, a makeshift pool. The day Nonso died was mild; there was drizzle in the morning, lukewarm sun in the afternoon, and, in the evening, Nonso's death. Grandmama screamed at him—at his limp body—saying *i laputago m,* that he had betrayed her, asking him who would carry on the Nnabuisi name now, who would protect the family lineage.

The neighbors came over when they heard her. It was the woman from the house across the road—the one whose dog rummaged in Grandmama's dustbin in the mornings—who coaxed the American phone number from your numb lips and called your mother. It was also that neighbor who unclasped your and Dozie's hands, made you sit down, and gave you some water. The neighbor tried, too, to hold you close so you would not hear Grandmama as she talked to your mother on the phone, but you slid away from the woman, closer to the phone. Grandmama and your mother were focused on Nonso's body, rather than his death. Your mother was insisting that Nonso's body be flown back to America right away and Grandmama was repeating your mother's words and shaking her head. Madness lurked in her eyes.

You knew Grandmama had never liked your mother. (You had heard Grandmama say this some summers before to her friend—That black American woman has tied up my son and put him in her pocket.) But watching Grandmama on the phone, you understood that she and your mother were united. You were sure your mother had the same red madness in her eyes.

When you talked to your mother, her voice echoed over the line in a way it had never done all the years before when you and Nonso spent summers with Grandmama. Are you all right? she kept asking you. Are you all right? She sounded fearful, as though she suspected that you *were* all right, despite Nonso's death. You played with the phone wire and said little. She said she would send word to your father, although he was some-where in the woods attending a Black Arts festival where there were no phones or radios. Finally she sobbed a harsh sob, a sob like the bark of a dog, before she told you everything would be fine and she was going to arrange for Nonso's body to be flown back. It made you think of her laugh, a *ho-ho-ho* laugh that started deep inside her belly and did not soften as it came up and did not suit her willowy body at all. When she went into Nonso's room to say good night, she always came out laughing that laugh. Most times, you pressed your palms to your ears to keep the sound out, and kept your palms pressed to your ears even when she came into your room to say Good night, dar-ling, sleep well. She never left your room with that laugh.

After the phone call, Grandmama lay stretched out with her back on the floor, eyes unblinking, rolling from side to side, as though she were playing some sort of silly game. She said it was wrong to fly Nonso's body back to America, that his spirit would always hover here. He belonged to this hard earth that had failed to absorb the shock of his fall. He belonged to the trees here, one of which had let go of him. You sat and watched her and at first you wished she would get up and take you in her arms, then you wished she wouldn't.

It has been eighteen years and the trees in Grandmama's yard look unchanged; they still reach out and hug one another, still cast shadows over the yard. But everything else seems smaller: the house, the garden at the back, the water tank copper-colored from rust. Even Grandmama's grave in the backyard looks tiny, and you imagine her body being crumpled to fit a small coffin. The grave is covered with a thin coat of cement; the soil around it is freshly dug and you stand next to it and picture it in ten years' time, untended, tangled weeds covering the cement, choking the grave.

Dozie is watching you. At the airport, he had hugged you cautiously, said welcome and what a surprise that you came back, and you stared at his face for a long time in the busy, shuffling lounge until he looked away, his eyes brown and sad like those of your friend's poodle. You didn't need that look, though, to know that the secret of how Nonso died was safe with Dozie, had always been safe with Dozie. As he drove to Grandmama's house, he asked about your mother and you told him that your mother lived in California now; you did not mention that it was in a commune among people with shaved heads and pierced breasts or that when she called, you always hung up while she was still speaking.

You move toward the avocado tree. Dozie is still watching you and you look at him and try to remember the love that clogged you up so fully that summer you were ten, that made you hold on tight to Dozie's hand the afternoon after Nonso died, when Dozie's mother, your aunty Mgbechibelije, came to take him away. There is a gentle sorrow in the lines across his forehead, a melancholy in the way he stands with his arms by his sides. You suddenly wonder if he longed, too, like you did. You never knew what was beneath his quiet smile, beneath the times he would sit so still that the fruit flies perched on his arms, beneath the pictures he gave you and the birds he kept in a cardboard cage, petting them until they died. You wonder what, if anything, he felt about being the wrong grandson, the one who did not bear the Nnabuisi name.

You reach out to touch the trunk of the avocado tree; just as Dozie starts to say something, startling you because you think he is going to bring up Nonso's death, but he tells you that he never imagined that you would come back to say goodbye to Grandmama because he knew how much you hated her. That word—"hate"—hangs in the air between you both like an accusation. You want to say that when he called you in New York, the first time you were hearing his voice in eighteen years, to tell you that Grandmama had died—I thought you would want to know, were his words—you leaned on your office desk, your legs turning molten, a lifetime of silence collapsing, and it was not Grandmama you thought of, it was Nonso, and it was him, Dozie, and it was the avocado tree and it was that humid summer in the amoral kingdom of your childhood and it was all the things you had not allowed yourself to think about, that you had flattened to a thin sheet and tucked away.

But instead you say nothing and press your palms deep into the rough trunk of the tree. The pain soothes you. You remember eating the avocados; you liked yours with salt and Nonso didn't like his with salt and Grandmama always clucked and said you did not know what was good when you said the unsalted avocado nauseated you.

. . .

At Nonso's funeral in a cold cemetery in Virginia with tomb-stones jutting out obscenely, your mother was in faded black from head to toe, even a veil, and it made her cinnamon skin glow. Your father stood away from both of you, in his usual dashiki, milk-colored cowries coiled round his neck. He looked as if he were not family, as if he were one of the guests who sniffled loudly and later asked your mother in hushed tones exactly how Nonso had died, exactly how he had fallen from one of the trees he had climbed since he was a toddler.

Your mother said nothing to them, all those people who asked questions. She said nothing to you, either, about Nonso, not even when she cleaned up his room and packed his things. She did not ask if you wanted to keep anything, and you were relieved. You did not want to have any of his books with his handwriting that your mother said was neater than typewritten sentences. You did not want his photographs of pigeons in the park that your father said showed so much promise for a child. You did not want his paintings, which were mere copies of your father's only in different colors. Or his clothes. Or his stamp collection.

Your mother brought Nonso up, finally, three months after his funeral, when she told you about the divorce. She said the divorce was not about Nonso, that she and your father had long been growing apart. (Your father was in Zanzibar then; he had left right after Nonso's funeral.) Then your mother asked: How did Nonso die?

You still wonder how those words tumbled out of your mouth. You still do not recognize the clear-eyed child that you were. Maybe it was because of the way she said the divorce was not about Nonso—as though Nonso was the only one capable of being a reason, as though you were not in the running. Or maybe it was simply that you felt the burning desire that you still feel sometimes, the need to smooth out wrinkles, to flatten things you find too bumpy. You told your mother, with your tone suitably reluctant, that Grandmama had asked Nonso to climb to the highest branch of the avocado tree to show her how much of a man he was. Then she frightened him—it was a joke, you assured your mother—by telling him that there was a snake, the *echi eteka,* on the branch close to him. She asked him not to move. Of course he moved and slipped off the branch, and when he landed, the sound was like many fruits falling at the same time. A dull, final plop. Grandmama stood there and stared at him and then started to shout at him about how he was the only son, how he had betrayed the lineage by dying, how the ancestors would be displeased. He was breathing, you told your mother. He was breathing when he fell but Grandmama just stood there and shouted at his broken body until he died.

Your mother started to scream. And you wondered if people screamed in that crazed way when they had just chosen to reject truth. She knew well enough that Nonso had hit his head on a stone and died on the spot—she had seen his body, his cracked head. But she chose to believe Nonso was alive after he fell. She cried, howled, and cursed the day she set eyes on your father at the first exhibition of his work. Then she called him, you heard her shouting on the phone: Your mother is responsible! She panicked him and made him fall! She could have done something afterwards but instead she stood there like the stupid fetish African woman that she is and let him die!

Your father talked to you afterwards, and said he understood how hard it was for you but you had to be careful what you said so that you didn't cause more hurt. And you thought about his words—Be careful what you say—and wondered if he knew you were lying.

That summer, eighteen years ago, was the summer of your first self-realization. The summer you knew that something had to happen to Nonso, so that you could survive. Even at ten you knew that some people can take up too much space by simply being, that by existing, some people can stifle others. The idea of scaring Nonso with the *echi eteka* was yours alone. But you explained it to Dozie, that you both needed Nonso to get hurt—maybe maim him, maybe twist his legs. You wanted to mar the perfection of his lithe body, to make him less lovable, less able to do all that he did. Less able to take up your space. Dozie said nothing and instead drew a picture of you with your eyes in the shape of stars.

Grandmama was inside cooking and Dozie was standing silently close to you, your shoulders touching, when you suggested Nonso climb to the top of the avocado tree. It was easy to get him to; you only had to remind him that you were the better climber. And you really were the better climber, you could scale a tree, any tree, in seconds—you were better at the things that did not need to be taught, the things that Grandmama could not teach him. You asked him to go first, to see if he could get to the topmost branch of the avocado before you followed. The branches were weak, and Nonso was heavier than you. Heavy from all the food Grandmama made him eat. Eat a little more, she would say often. Who do you think I made it for? As though you were not there. Sometimes she would pat your back and say in Igbo, It's good you are learning, *nne,* this is how you will take care of your husband one day.

Nonso climbed the tree. Higher and higher. You waited till

he was nearly at the top, till his legs hesitated before inching farther up. You waited for that short moment when he was between motions. An open moment, a moment you saw the blueness of everything, of life itself—the pure azure of one of your father's paintings, of opportunity, of a sky washed clean by a morning shower. Then you screamed. "A snake! It's the *echi eteka*! A snake!" You were not sure whether to say that the snake was on a branch close to him, or sliding up the trunk. But it didn't matter because, in those few seconds, Nonso looked down at you and let go, his foot slipping, his arms freeing themselves. Or maybe the tree simply shrugged Nonso off.

You don't remember now how long you stayed looking at Nonso before you went in to call Grandmama, Dozie all the time silent beside you.

Dozie's word—"hate"—floats around in your head now. Hate. Hate. Hate. The word makes it difficult to breathe, the same way it was difficult to breathe when you waited, those months after Nonso died, for your mother to notice that you had a voice pure like water and legs like elastic bands, for your mother to end her good-night visits to your room with that deep *ho-ho-ho* laugh. Instead she held you too gingerly while saying good night, always speaking in whispers, and you started to avoid her kisses by faking coughs and sneezes. Year after year as she moved you from state to state, lighting red candles in her bedroom, banning all talk of Nigeria or of Grandmama, refusing to let you see your father, she never again laughed that laugh.

Dozie speaks now, tells you that he began to dream of Nonso a few years ago, dreams in which Nonso is older and taller than him, and you hear fruit fall from a tree nearby and you ask him without turning around, What did you want, that summer, what did you want?

You do not know when Dozie moves, when he stands behind you, so close that you smell the citrus on him, perhaps he peeled an orange and did not wash his hands afterwards. He turns you around and looks at you and you look at him and there are fine lines on his forehead and a new harshness in his eyes. He tells you it did not occur to him to want because what mattered was what you wanted. There is a long silence while you watch the column of black ants making its way up the trunk, each ant carrying a bit of white fluff, creating a black-and-white pattern. He asks you if you dreamed the way he did and you say no, your eyes avoiding his, and he turns away from you. You want to tell him about the pain in your chest and the emptiness in your ears and the roiling air after his phone call, about the doors flung open, about the flattened things that popped out, but he is walking away. And you are weeping, standing alone under the avocado tree.

THE HEADSTRONG
HISTORIAN

Many years after her husband died, Nwamgba still closed her eyes from time to time to relive his nightly visits to her hut and the mornings after, when she would walk to the stream humming a song, thinking of the smoky scent of him, the firmness of his weight, those secrets she shared with herself, and feeling as if she were surrounded by light. Other memories of Obierika remained clear—his stubby fingers curled around his flute when he played in the evenings, his delight when she set down his bowls of food, his sweaty back when he returned with baskets filled with fresh clay for her pottery. From the moment she first saw him at a wrestling match, both of them staring and staring at each other, both of them too young, her waist not yet wearing the menstruation cloth, she had believed with a quiet stubbornness that her chi and his chi had destined their marriage, and so when he came to her father a few years later bringing pots of palm wine and accompanied by his relatives, she told her mother that this was the man she would marry. Her mother was aghast. Did Nwambga not know that Obierika was an only child, that his late father had been an only child whose wives had lost pregnancies and buried babies? Perhaps somebody in their family had committed the taboo of selling a girl into slavery and the earth god Ani was visiting misfortune on them. Nwamgba ignored her mother. She went into her father's *obi* and told him she would run away from any other man's house if she was not allowed to marry Obierika. Her father found her exhausting, this sharp-tongued, head-strong daughter who had once wrestled her brother to the ground. (After which her father had warned everybody not to let the news leave the compound that the girl had thrown a boy.) He, too, was concerned about the infertility in Obierika's family, but it was not a bad family: Obierika's late father had taken the *ozo* title; Obierika was already giving out his seed yams to sharecroppers. Nwamgba would not do badly if she married him. Besides, it was better that he let her go with the man she chose, to save himself years of trouble when she would keep returning home after confrontations with in-laws. And so he gave his blessing and she smiled and called him by his praise name.

To pay her bride price, Obierika came with two maternal cousins, Okafo and Okoye, who were like brothers to him. Nwamgba loathed them at first sight. She saw a grasping envy in their eyes that afternoon as they drank palm wine in her father's *obi,* and in the following years, years in which Obierika took titles and widened his compound and sold his yams to strangers from afar, she saw their envy blacken. But she tolerated them, because they mattered to Obierika, because he pretended not to notice that they didn't work but came to him for yams and chickens, because he wanted to imagine that he had

brothers. It was they who urged him, after her third miscarriage, to marry another wife. Obierika told them he would
give it some thought but when he and Nwamgba were alone
in her hut at night, he told her that he was sure they would
have a home full of children, and that he would not marry
another wife until they were old, so that they would have
somebody to care for them. She thought this strange of him, a
prosperous man with only one wife, and she worried more
than he did about their childlessness, about the songs that people sang, melodious mean-spirited words: *She has sold her womb.
She has eaten his penis. He plays his flute and hands over his wealth
to her.*

Once, at a moonlight gathering, the square full of women
telling stories and learning new dances, a group of girls saw
Nwamgba and began to sing, their aggressive breasts pointing at her. She stopped and asked whether they would mind
singing a little louder so that she could hear the words and then
show them who was the greater of two tortoises. They stopped
singing. She enjoyed their fear, the way they backed away from
her, but it was then that she decided to find a wife for Obierika
herself.

Nwamgba liked going to the Oyi stream, untying her wrapper
from her waist and walking down the slope to the silvery rush
of water that burst out from a rock. The waters of Oyi were
fresher than those of the other stream, Ogalanya, or perhaps it
was simply that she felt comforted by the shrine of the Oyi
goddess, tucked away in a corner; as a child she had learned that
Oyi was the protector of women, the reason women were not
to be sold into slavery. Her closest friend, Ayaju, was already at
the stream, and as Nwamgba helped her raise her pot to her

head, she asked Ayaju who might be a good second wife for Obierika.

She and Ayaju had grown up together and married men from the same clan. The difference between them, though, was that Ayaju was of slave descent; her father had been brought as a slave after a war. Ayaju did not care for her husband, Okenwa, who she said resembled and smelled like a rat, but her marriage prospects had been limited; no man from a freeborn family would have come for her hand. Ayaju's long-limbed, quick-moving body spoke of her many trading journeys; she had traveled even beyond Onicha. It was she who had first brought tales of the strange customs of the Igala and Edo traders, she who first told of the white-skinned men who arrived in Onicha with mirrors and fabrics and the biggest guns the people of those parts had ever seen. This cosmopolitanism earned her respect, and she was the only person of slave descent who talked loudly at the Women's Council, the only person who had answers for everything.

And so she promptly suggested, for Obierika's second wife, the young girl from the Okonkwo family; the girl had beautiful wide hips and was respectful, nothing like the young girls of today with their heads full of nonsense. As they walked home from the stream, Ayaju said that perhaps Nwamgba should do what other women in her situation did—take a lover and get pregnant in order to continue Obierika's lineage. Nwamgba's retort was sharp, because she did not like Ayaju's tone, which suggested that Obierika was impotent, and as if in response to her thoughts she felt a furious stab in her back and knew that she was pregnant again, but she said nothing, because she knew, too, that she would lose the baby again.

Her miscarriage happened a few weeks later, lumpy blood running down her legs. Obierika comforted her and suggested they go to the famous oracle, Kisa, as soon as she was well enough for the half day's journey. After the *dibia* had consulted the oracle, Nwamgba cringed at the thought of sacrificing a whole cow; Obierika certainly had greedy ancestors. But they did the ritual cleansings and the sacrifices, and when she suggested he go and see the Okonkwo family about their daughter, he delayed and delayed until another sharp pain spliced her back; and months later, she was lying on a pile of freshly washed banana leaves behind her hut, straining and pushing until the baby slipped out.

They named him Anikwenwa: the earth god Ani had finally granted a child. He was dark and solidly built and had Obierika's happy curiosity. Obierika took him to pick medicinal herbs, to collect clay for Nwamgba's pottery, to twist yam vines at the farm. Obierika's cousins Okafo and Okoye visited too often. They marveled at how well Anikwenwa played the flute, how quickly he was learning poetry and wrestling moves from his father, but Nwamgba saw the glowing malevolence that their smiles could not hide. She feared for her child and her husband, and when Obierika died—a man who had been hearty and laughing and drinking palm wine moments before he slumped—she knew that they had killed him with medicine. She clung to his corpse until a neighbor slapped her to make her let go; she lay in the cold ash for days; she tore at the patterns shaved into her hair. Obierika's death left her with an unending despair. She thought often of the woman who, after her tenth successive child died, had gone to her backyard and hanged herself on a kola tree. But she would not do it, because of Anikwenwa.

Later, she wished she had insisted that his cousins drink Obierika's *mmili ozu* before the oracle. She had witnessed this once, when a wealthy man died and his family insisted his rival drink his *mmili ozu*. Nwamgba had watched the unmarried woman take a cupped leaf full of water, touch it to the dead man's body, all the time speaking solemnly, and give the leaf-cup to the accused man. He drank. Everyone watched to make sure he swallowed, a grave silence in the air because they knew that if he was guilty he would die. He died days later, and his family lowered their heads in shame and Nwamgba felt strangely shaken by it all. She should have insisted on this with Obierika's cousins, but she had been blinded by grief and now Obierika was buried and it was too late.

His cousins, during the funeral, took his ivory tusk, claiming that the trappings of titles went to brothers and not to sons. It was when they emptied his barn of yams and led away the adult goats in his pen that she confronted them, shouting, and when they brushed her aside, she waited until evening and then walked around the clan singing about their wicked-ness, the abominations they were heaping on the land by cheating a widow, until the elders asked them to leave her alone. She complained to the Women's Council, and twenty women went at night to Okafo and Okoye's home, brandishing pestles, warning them to leave Nwamgba alone. Members of Obierika's age grade, too, told them to leave her alone. But Nwamgba knew those grasping cousins would never really stop. She dreamed of killing them. She certainly could—those weaklings who had spent their lives scrounging off Obierika instead of working—but of course she would be banished and there would be nobody to care for her son. So she took Anikwenwa on long walks, telling him that the land from that palm tree to that plantain tree was theirs, that his grandfather had passed it on to his father. She told him the same things over and over, even though he looked bored and bewildered, and she did not let him go and play at moonlight unless she was watching.

Ayaju came back from a trading journey with another story: the women in Onicha were complaining about the white men. They had welcomed the white men's trading station, but now the white men wanted to tell them how to trade, and when the elders of Agueke, a clan of Onicha, refused to place their thumbs on a paper, the white men came at night with their normal-men helpers and razed the village. There was nothing left. Nwamgba did not understand. What sort of guns did these white men have? Ayaju laughed and said their guns were nothing like the rusty thing her own husband owned. Some white men were visiting different clans, asking parents to send their children to school, and she had decided to send Azuka, the son who was laziest on the farm, because although she was respected and wealthy, she was still of slave descent, her sons still barred from taking titles. She wanted Azuka to learn the ways of these foreigners, since people ruled over others not because they were better people but because they had better guns; after all, her own father would not have been brought as a slave if his clan had been as well armed as Nwamgba's clan. As Nwamgba listened to her friend, she dreamed of killing Obierika's cousins with the white men's guns.

The day that the white men visited her clan, Nwamgba left the pot she was about to put in her oven, took Anikwenwa and her girl apprentices, and hurried to the square. She was at first disappointed by the ordinariness of the two white men; they were harmless-looking, the color of albinos, with frail and slender limbs. Their companions were normal men, but there was something foreign about them, too, and only one spoke a strangely accented Igbo. He said that he was from Elele; the other normal men were from Sierra Leone, and the white men from France, far across the sea. They were all of the Holy Ghost Congregation; they had arrived in Onicha in 1885 and were building their school and church there. Nwamgba was first to ask a question: Had they brought their guns by any chance, the ones used to destroy the people of Agueke, and could she see one? The man said unhappily that it was the soldiers of the British government and merchants of the Royal Niger Company who destroyed villages; they, instead, brought good news. He spoke about their god, who had come to the world to die, and who had a son but no wife, and who was three but also one. Many of the people around Nwamgba laughed loudly. Some walked away, because they had imagined that the white man was full of wisdom. Others stayed and offered cool bowls of water.

Weeks later, Ayaju brought another story: the white men had set up a courthouse in Onicha where they judged disputes. They had indeed come to stay. For the first time, Nwamgba doubted her friend. Surely the people of Onicha had their own courts. The clan next to Nwamgba's, for example, held its courts only during the new yam festival, so that people's rancor grew while they awaited justice. A stupid system, Nwamgba thought, but surely everyone had one. Ayaju laughed and told Nwamgba again that people ruled others when they had better guns. Her son was already learning about these foreign ways, and perhaps Anikwenwa should, too. Nwamgba refused. It was unthinkable that her only son, her single eye, should be given to the white men, never mind how superior their guns might be.

Three events, in the following years, caused Nwamgba to change her mind. The first was that Obierika's cousins took over a large piece of land and told the elders that they were farming it for her, a woman who had emasculated their dead brother and now refused to remarry even though suitors were coming and her breasts were still round. The elders sided with them. The second was that Ayaju told a story of two people who took a land case to the white men's court; the first man was lying but could speak the white men's language, while the second man, the rightful owner of the land, could not, and so he lost his case, was beaten and locked up and ordered to give up his land. The third was the story of the boy Iroegbunam, who had gone missing many years ago and then suddenly reappeared, a grown man, his widowed mother mute with shock at his story: a neighbor, whom his father often shouted down at age-grade meetings, had abducted him when his mother was at the market and taken him to the Aro slave dealers, who looked him over and complained that the wound on his leg would reduce his price. Then he and some others were tied together by the hands. forming a long human column, and he was hit with a stick and asked to walk faster. There was only one woman among them. She shouted herself hoarse, telling the abductors that they were heartless, that her spirit would torment them and their children, that she knew she was to be sold to the white man, and did they not know that the white man's slavery was very different, that people were treated like goats, taken on large ships a long way away and eventually eaten?

Iroegbunam walked and walked and walked, his feet bloodied, his body numb, with a little water poured into his mouth from time to time, until all he could remember later was the smell of dust. Finally they stopped at a coastal clan, where a man spoke a nearly incomprehensible Igbo, but Iroegbunam made out enough to understand that another man, who was to sell the abductees to the white people on the ship, had gone up to bargain with the white people but had himself been kidnapped. There were loud arguments, scuffling; some of the abductees yanked at the ropes and Iroegbunam passed out. He awoke to find a white man rubbing his feet with oil, and at first he was terrified, certain that he was being prepared for the white man's meal. But this was a different kind of white man, a missionary who bought slaves only to free them, and he took Iroegbunam to live with him and trained him to be a Christian missionary.

Iroegbunam's story haunted Nwamgba, because this, she was sure, was the way Obierika's cousins were likely to get rid of her son. Killing him was too dangerous, the risk of misfortunes from the oracle too high, but they would be able to sell him as long as they had strong medicine to protect themselves. She was struck, too, by how Iroegbunam lapsed into the white man's language from time to time. It sounded nasal and disgusting. Nwamgba had no desire to speak such a thing herself, but she was suddenly determined that Anikwenwa would speak it well enough to go to the white men's court with Obierika's cousins and defeat them and take control of what was his. And so, shortly after Iroegbunam's return, she told Ayaju that she wanted to take her son to school.

They went first to the Anglican mission. The classroom had more girls than boys—a few curious boys wandered in with their catapults and then wandered out. The students sat with slates on their laps while the teacher stood in front of them, holding a big cane, telling them a story about a man who transformed a bowl of water into wine. Nwamgba was impressed by the teacher's spectacles, and she thought that the man in the story must have had fairly powerful medicine to be able to transform water into wine. But when the girls were separated and a woman teacher came to teach them how to sew, Nwamgba found this silly; in her clan girls learned to make pottery and a man sewed cloth. What dissuaded her completely about the school, however, was that the instruction was done in Igbo. Nwamgba asked the first teacher why. He said that of course the students were taught English—he held up the English primer—but children learned best in their own language, and the children in the white men's land were taught in their own language, too. Nwamgba turned to leave. The teacher stood in her way and told her that the Catholic missionaries were harsh and did not have the best interests of the natives at heart. Nwamgba was amused by these foreigners, who did not seem to know that one must, in front of strangers, pretend to have unity. But she had come in search of English, and so she walked past him and went to the Catholic mission.

Father Shanahan told her that Anikwenwa would have to take an English name, because it was not possible to be baptized with a heathen name. She agreed easily. His name was Anikwenwa as far as she was concerned; if they wanted to name him something she could not pronounce before teaching him their language, she did not mind at all. All that mattered was that he learn enough of the language to fight his father's cousins. Father Shanahan looked at Anikwenwa, a dark-skinned, well-muscled child, and guessed that he was about twelve, although he found it difficult to estimate the ages of these people; sometimes a mere boy would look like a man, nothing like in Eastern Africa, where he had previously worked and where the natives tended to be slender, less confusingly muscular. As he poured some water on the boy's head, he said, "Michael, I baptize you in the name of the Father and of the Son and of the Holy Spirit."

He gave the boy a singlet and a pair of shorts, because the people of the living God did not walk around naked, and he tried to preach to the boy's mother, but she looked at him as if he were a child who did not know any better. There was something troublingly assertive about her, something he had seen in many women here; there was much potential to be harnessed if their wildness could be tamed. This Nwamgba would make a marvelous missionary among the women. He watched her leave. There was a grace in her straight back, and she, unlike others, had not spent too much time going round and round in her speech. It infuriated him, their overlong talk and circuitous proverbs, their never getting to the point, but he was determined to excel here; it was the reason he had joined the Holy Ghost Congregation, whose special vocation was the redemption of black heathens.

Nwamgba was alarmed by how indiscriminately the missionaries flogged students—for being late, for being lazy, for being slow, for being idle. And once, as Anikwenwa told her, Father Lutz had put metal cuffs around a girl's wrists to teach her a lesson about lying, all the time saying in Igbo—for Father Lutz spoke a broken brand of Igbo—that native parents pampered their children too much, that teaching the Gospel also meant teaching proper discipline. The first weekend Anikwenwa came home, Nwamgba saw angry welts on his back. She tightened her wrapper on her waist and went to the school. She told the teacher that she would gouge out the eyes of everyone at the mission if they ever did that to him again. She knew that Anikwenwa did not want to go to school, and she told him that it was only for a year or two, so that he would learn English, and although the mission people told her not to come so often, she insistently came every weekend to take him home. Anikwenwa always took off his clothes even before they left the mission compound. He disliked the shorts and shirt that made him sweat, the fabric that was itchy around his armpits. He disliked, too, being in the same class as old men and missing out on wrestling contests.

Perhaps it was because he began to notice the admiring glances his clothes brought in the clan but Anikwenwa's attitude to school slowly changed. Nwamgba first noticed this when some of the other boys with whom he swept the village square complained that he no longer did his share because he was at school, and Anikwenwa said something in English, something sharp-sounding, which shut them up and filled Nwamgba with an indulgent pride. Her pride turned to a vague worry when she noticed that the curiosity in his eyes had diminished. There was a new ponderousness in him, as if he had suddenly found himself bearing the weight of a too-heavy world. He stared at things for too long. He stopped eating her food, because, he said, it was sacrificed to idols. He told her to tie her wrapper around her chest instead of her waist, because her nakedness was sinful. She looked at him, amused by his earnestness, but worried nonetheless, and asked why he had only just begun to notice her nakedness.

When it was time for his *ima mmuo* ceremony, he said he would not participate, because it was a heathen custom for boys to be initiated into the world of spirits, a custom that Father

Shanahan had said would have to stop. Nwamgba roughly yanked his ear and told him that a foreign albino could not determine when their customs would change, so until the clan itself decided that the initiation would stop, he would participate or else he would tell her whether he was her son or the white man's son. Anikwenwa reluctantly agreed, but as he was taken away with a group of boys, she noticed that he lacked their excitement. His sadness saddened her. She felt her son slipping away from her, and yet she was proud that he was learning so much, that he could become a court interpreter or a letter writer, and that with Father Lutz's help he had brought home some papers that showed that their lands belonged to him and his mother. Her proudest moment was when he went to his father's cousins Okafo and Okoye and asked for his father's ivory tusk back. And they gave it to him.

Nwamgba knew that her son now inhabited a mental space that was foreign to her. He told her that he was going to Lagos to learn how to be a teacher, and even as she screamed—How can you leave me? Who will bury me when I die?—she knew he would go. She did not see him for many years, years during which his father's cousin Okafo died. She often consulted the oracle to ask whether Anikwenwa was still alive; the *dibia* admonished her and sent her away, because of course he was alive. At last Anikwenwa returned, in the year that the clan banned all dogs after a dog killed a member of the Mmangala age grade, the age grade to which Anikwenwa would have belonged if he had not said that such things were devilish.

Nwamgba said nothing when he announced that he had been appointed catechist at the new mission. She was sharpening her *aguba* on the palm of her hand, about to shave patterns in the hair of a little girl, and she continued to do so—*flick-flick-flick*—while Anikwenwa talked about winning souls in their clan. The plate of breadfruit seeds she had offered him was untouched—he no longer ate anything at all of hers—and she looked at him, this man wearing trousers, and a rosary around his neck, and wondered whether she had meddled with his destiny. Was this what his chi had ordained for him, this life in which he was like a person diligently acting a bizarre pantomime?

The day that he told her about the woman he would marry, she was not surprised. He did not do it as it was done, did not consult people to ask about the bride's family, but simply said that somebody at the mission had seen a suitable young woman from Ifite Ukpo and the suitable young woman would be taken to the Sisters of the Holy Rosary in Onicha to learn how to be a good Christian wife. Nwamgba was sick with malaria on that day, lying on her mud bed, rubbing her aching joints, and she asked Anikwenwa the young woman's name. Anikwenwa said it was Agnes. Nwamgba asked for the young woman's real name. Anikwenwa cleared his throat and said she had been called Mgbeke before she became a Christian, and Nwamgba asked whether Mgbeke would at least do the confession ceremony even if Anikwenwa would not follow the other marriage rites of their clan. He shook his head furiously and told her that the confession made by a woman before marriage, in which she, surrounded by female relatives, swore that no man had touched her since her husband had declared his interest, was sinful, because Christian wives should not have been touched *at all*.

The marriage ceremony in church was laughably strange, but Nwamgba bore it silently and told herself that she would die soon and join Obierika and be free of a world that increasingly made no sense. She was determined to dislike her son's wife, but Mgbeke was difficult to dislike; she was small-waisted and gentle, eager to please the man to whom she was married, eager to please everyone, quick to cry, apologetic about things over which she had no control. And so, instead, Nwamgba pitied her. Mgbeke often visited Nwamgba in tears, saying that Anikwenwa had refused to eat dinner because he was upset with her or that Anikwenwa had banned her from going to a friend's Anglican wedding because Anglicans did not preach the truth, and Nwamgba would silently carve designs on her pottery while Mgbeke cried, uncertain of how to handle a woman crying about things that did not deserve tears.

Mgbeke was called "missus" by everyone, even the non-Christians, all of whom respected the catechist's wife, but on the day she went to the Oyi stream and refused to remove her clothes because she was a Christian, the women of the clan, outraged that she dared to disrespect the goddess, beat her and dumped her at the grove. The news spread quickly. Missus had been harassed. Anikwenwa threatened to lock up all the elders if his wife was treated that way again, but Father O'Donnell, on his next trek from his station in Onicha, visited the elders and apologized on Mgbeke's behalf and asked whether perhaps Christian women could be allowed to fetch water fully clothed. The elders refused—if one wanted Oyi's waters, then one had to follow Oyi's rules—but they were courteous to Father O'Donnell, who listened to them and did not behave like their own son Anikwenwa.

Nwamgba was ashamed of her son, irritated with his wife, upset by their rarefied life in which they treated non-Christians as if they had smallpox, but she held out her hope for a grandchild; she prayed and sacrificed for Mgbeke to have a boy, because it would be Obierika come back and would bring a semblance of sense back into her world. She did not know of Mgbeke's first or second miscarriage, it was only after the third that Mgbeke, sniffling and blowing her nose, told her. They had to consult the oracle, as this was a family misfortune, Nwamgba said, but Mgbeke's eyes widened with fear. Michael would be very angry if he ever heard of this oracle suggestion. Nwamgba, who still found it difficult to remember that Michael was Anikwenwa, went to the oracle herself, and afterwards thought it ludicrous how even the gods had changed and no longer asked for palm wine but for gin. Had they converted, too?

A few months later, Mgbeke visited, smiling, bringing a covered bowl of one of those concoctions that Nwamgba found inedible, and Nwamgba knew that her chi was still wide awake and that her daughter-in-law was pregnant. Anikwenwa had decreed that Mgbeke would have the baby at the mission in Onicha, but the gods had different plans and she went into early labor on a rainy afternoon; somebody ran in the drenching rain to Nwamgba's hut to call her. It was a boy. Father O'Donnell baptized him Peter, but Nwamgba called him Nnamdi, because she believed he was Obierika come back. She sang to him, and when he cried she pushed her dried-up nipple into his mouth, but try as she might, she did not feel the spirit of her magnificent husband Obierika. Mgbeke had three more miscarriages and Nwamgba went to the oracle many times until a pregnancy stayed and the second baby was born, this time at the mission in Onicha. A girl. From the moment Nwamgba held her, the baby's bright eyes delightfully focused on her, she knew that it was the spirit of Obierika that had returned; odd, to have come in a girl, but who could predict the ways of the ancestors? Father O'Donnell baptized her Grace, but Nwamgba called her Afamefuna, "My Name Will Not Be Lost," and was thrilled by the child's solemn interest in her poetry and her stories, the teenager's keen watchfulness as Nwamgba struggled to make pottery with newly shaky hands. But Nwamgba was not thrilled that Afamefuna was to go away to secondary school (Peter was already living with the priests in Onicha), because she feared that, at boarding school, the new ways would dissolve her granddaughter's fighting spirit and replace it either with an incurious rigidity, like Anikwenwa's, or a limp helplessness, like Mgbeke's.

The year that Afamefuna left for secondary school in Onicha, Nwamgba felt as if a lamp had been blown out on a moonless night. It was a strange year, the year that darkness suddenly descended on the land in the middle of the afternoon, and when Nwamgba felt the deep-seated ache in her joints, she knew her end was near. She lay on her bed gasping for breath, while Anikwenwa pleaded with her to be baptized and anointed so that he could hold a Christian funeral for her, as he could not participate in a heathen ceremony. Nwamgba told him that if he dared to bring anybody to rub some filthy oil on her, she would slap that person with her last strength. All she wanted was to see Afamefuna before she joined the ancestors, but Anikwenwa said that Grace was taking exams in school and could not come home. But she came. Nwamgba heard the squeaky swing of her door and there was Afamefuna, her granddaughter who had come on her own from Onicha because she had been unable to sleep for days, her restless spirit urging her home. Grace put down her schoolbag, inside of which was her textbook with a chapter called "The Pacification of the Primitive Tribes of Southern Nigeria," by an administrator from Worcestershire who had lived among them for seven years.

It was Grace who would read about these savages, titillated by their curious and meaningless customs, not connecting them to herself until her teacher, Sister Maureen, told her she could not refer to the call-and-response her grandmother had taught her as poetry because primitive tribes did not have poetry. It was Grace who would laugh loudly until Sister Maureen took her to detention and then summoned her father, who slapped Grace in front of the teachers to show them how well he disciplined his children. It was Grace who would nurse a deep scorn for her father for years, spending holidays working as a maid in Onicha so as to avoid the sanctimonies, the dour certainties, of her parents and brother. It was Grace who, after graduating from secondary school, would teach elementary school in Agueke, where people told stories of the destruction of their village years before by the white men's guns, stories she was not sure she believed, because they also told stories of mermaids appearing from the River Niger holding wads of crisp cash. It was Grace who, as one of the few women at the University College in Ibadan in 1950, would change her degree from chemistry to history after she heard, while drinking tea at the home of a friend, the story of Mr. Gboyega. The eminent Mr. Gboyega, a chocolate-skinned Nigerian, educated in London, distinguished expert on the history of the British Empire, had resigned in disgust when the West African Examinations Council began talking of adding African history to the curriculum, because he was appalled that African history would even be considered a subject. Grace would ponder this story for a long time, with great sadness, and it would cause her to make a clear link between education and dignity, between the hard, obvious things that are printed in books and the soft, subtle things that lodge themselves into the soul. It was Grace who would begin to rethink her own schooling—how lustily she had sung, on Empire Day, "God bless our Gracious King. Send him victorious, happy and glorious. Long to reign over us"; how she had puzzled over words like "wallpaper" and "dandelions" in her textbooks, unable to picture those things; how she had struggled with arithmetic problems that had to do with mixtures, because what was coffee and what was chicory and why did they have to be mixed? It was Grace who would begin to rethink her father's schooling and then hurry home to see him, his eyes watery with age, telling him she had not received all the letters she had ignored, saying amen when he prayed, pressing her lips against his forehead. It was Grace who, driving past Agueke on her way back, would become haunted by the image of a destroyed village and would go to London and to Paris and to Onicha, sifting through moldy files in archives, reimagining the lives and smells of her grandmother's world, for the book she would write called *Pacifying with Bullets: A Reclaimed History of Southern Nigeria*. It was Grace who, in a conversation about the early manuscript with her fiancé, George Chikadibia—stylish graduate of Kings College, Lagos; engineer-to-be; wearer of three-piece suits; expert ballroom dancer who often said that a grammar school without Latin was like a cup of tea without sugar—knew that the marriage would not last when George told her she was misguided to write about primitive culture instead of a worthwhile topic like African Alliances in the American-Soviet Tension. They would divorce in 1972, not because of the four miscarriages Grace had suffered but because she woke up sweating one night and realized that she would strangle him to death if she had to listen to one more rapturous monologue about his Cambridge days. It was Grace who, as she received faculty prizes, as she spoke to solemn-faced people at conferences about the Ijaw and Ibibio and Igbo and Efik peoples of South-

ern Nigeria, as she wrote reports for international organiza-
tions about commonsense things for which she nevertheless
received generous pay, would imagine her grandmother looking on and chuckling with great amusement. It was Grace who,
feeling an odd rootlessness in the later years of her life, surrounded by her awards, her friends, her garden of peerless roses,
would go to the courthouse in Lagos and officially change her
first name from Grace to Afamefuna.

But on that day as she sat at her grandmother's bedside in the
fading evening light, Grace was not contemplating her future.
She simply held her grandmother's hand, the palm thickened
from years of making pottery.

ACKNOWLEDGMENTS

Thank you to Sarah Chalfant, Robin Desser, and Mitzi Angel.

The following stories have been previously published:"Jumping Monkey Hill" in *Granta 95: Loved Ones;* "On Monday of Last Week" in *Granta 98: The Deep End;* "The Arrangers of Marriage" as "New Husband" in *Iowa Review;* "Cell One" and "The Headstrong Historian" in *The New Yorker;* "Imitation" in *Other Voices;* "The American Embassy" in *Prism International;* "The Thing Around Your Neck" in *Prospect 99;* "Tomorrow Is Too Far" in *Prospect 118;* "A Private Experience" in *Virginia Quarterly Review;* and "Ghosts" in *Zoetrope: All-Story.* "The American Embassy" also appeared in *The O. Henry Prize Stories 2003,* edited by Laura Furman (Anchor Books, 2003).

Chimamanda Ngozi Adichie grew up in Nigeria. Her work has been translated into thirty languages and has appeared in various publications, including *The New Yorker, Granta,* the *Financial Times,* and *Zoetrope.* Her story "The American Embassy" was included in *The O. Henry Prize Stories 2003.* Her most recent novel, *Half of a Yellow Sun,* won the Orange Prize and was a finalist for the National Book Critics Circle Award; it was a *New York Times* Notable Book and a *People* and *Black Issues Book Review* Best Book of the Year. Her first novel, *Purple Hibiscus,* won the Commonwealth Writers' Prize and the Hurston/Wright Legacy Award. A recipient of a 2008 MacArthur Foundation Fellowship, she divides her time between the United States and Nigeria.

A NOTE ON THE TYPE

This book was set in a version of the well-known Monotype face Bembo. This letter was cut for the celebrated Venetian printer Aldus Manutius by Francesco Griffo, and first used in Pietro Cardinal Bembo's *De Aetna* of 1495. The companion italic is an adaptation of the chancery script type designed by the calligrapher and printer Lodovico degli Arrighi.

Composed by Creative Graphics, Allentown, Pennsylvania
Printed and bound by R. R. Donnelley,
Harrisonburg, Virginia
Designed by Wesley Gott